MW01180910

Pieces of a Presidential Mind!

By Jay Bruce Barton

thanks to my family & friends
especially my siblings who
as mom said "we will still be
fighting & teasing each other
when we are in 80's"

This book is dedicated
to my Mom –
Virginia C. Leeper Barton
4/16/31 to 10/16/94
thanks for teaching your children
to love and appreciate the joy
of reading and the world
of books!

Cover Art is the
work of the very talented –
Heather Moser!

Preface

Tonight, December 9th, 2065, for the 100th time, "A Charlie Brown Christmas" aired on network television. How do I know the obscure fact that it is the 100th time? Well, it aired for the very first time on the night that I was born in 1965. You might say two classics were born that night. You would be wrong because I am anything but a classic in my opinion. However, on that night a century ago, I was born into an average American home, raised in an average small town in Ohio, and by some not so average events became the President of the United States of America.

I am very proud to say that I was an Average American who was able to reach the White House and serve this great nation of ours. I also believe that I was able to help put "We the People" back into the government. I hope that I made a difference.

Over the years since I served as President, I was approached many times by publishers, asking me to write my memoirs and every time, I said no. I said no because I just never wanted to take the time and because I actually never thought I had anything all that important to write.

However, as I sat here this evening getting ready to be 100 years old at 10:06pm, I decided that it was finally time to write my memoirs. I decided to put down on paper what I feel is important for the historians to know about me in the future since I want to set the record straight. I don't want others deciding what in my life was important and what things weren't important. I don't want a stranger deciding who influenced my thinking. Finally, I don't want some academic type person sitting in an ivory tower implying what I meant by this or what I meant by that. So if it isn't in this book it wasn't important. Also, I plan to write the facts – the good, the bad, and the ugly and nothing should be construed to mean anything other than what I write – despite any interpretations anyone else might make about my life and times.

So sit back, relax & prepare to be somewhat bored and hopefully somewhat amused by a very old and very stubborn ex-president who definitely is in his twilight years.

Chapter One – The Ancestors

I know what a lot of you are thinking as you see a title of "The Ancestors". You are thinking oh no this is either going to be really boring because it is going to be a whole lot of this person begat this person and this person begat this person or if you aren't thinking of this chapter in those terms, you are thinking here come all the stories of this old man's great great great great great grandfather who served in the American Revolution alongside George Washington. Along those lines, I assume that you would not want to hear if I had a great great great grandfather on my mother's side who was one of the greatest and wealthiest carpetbaggers to fleece the south after the Civil War. I also would assume that you wouldn't want to know of the long lost relatives who were Cherokee Indian warriors. Well the good news for all of you is that I will not talk of who begat who nor will you be hearing about wealthy &/or historically significant relatives (primarily because I don't know of any). Instead, the ancestors that I plan to speak of are the ancestors that I actually knew and these are the ones who actually had an influence on the man I was before, during and after my presidency. I also want to explain the gift that each of these individuals gave to me.

MOTHER

Like most sons will say, my mother was one of a kind and truly the best. She was born during the Great Depression and grew up in Canton, Ohio. She and her family were fortunate in so much as her father had a good job with the electric company and they never really suffered during the depression. They never lost their home and they never went hungry. Though she grew up in the 1930's and 40's during the Depression and the following years with World War II, life had its fun and exciting moments.

For example there was her pet alligator.

That story goes like this:

As a little girl, my mother, who lived on Barret Court in an average neighborhood of Canton, Ohio, was reading a magazine one day when she was 9 years old and she saw an ad to purchase alligators from Florida for fifty cents. She went to her father and asked for permission. Her father told her that it was probably a scam and that she would just lose her money. However, my mother was a very determined little girl who had decided that she was going to get herself an alligator so she talked her dad into it. He finally realized that it might be a good lesson if he let her do it because he would then be able to teach her not to be so trusting and that fathers are always right. So she mailed off the request with fifty cents that she had been saving in her piggy bank.

After a couple of weeks she started getting anxious and everyday she would wait on the front porch for the mailman and everyday she would ask "DO YOU HAVE MY ALLIGATOR?" Everyday the mailman would say "NO!"

So it went each day.

Finally after several days of this ritual the mailman's patience wore thin and he said "look little girl – stop asking me everyday about your alligator – when your alligator gets here, I will let you know that it is here!"

My mother kept waiting though – a silent vigil (because in those days children minded their elders and all that) – just hoping each day that it would be the day and the package would arrive from Florida.

Finally after about seven weeks the mailman came up the stairs of the front porch and handed my mother a package. "Here is your alligator little girl!" Well of course she went crazy screaming with delight and excitement. Her parents came to the porch wondering what exactly was going to be in this package. The mailman who didn't believe that there was even an alligator in the package sarcastically told her "well get on with it – open it up I want to see this alligator!"

So she opened it up and out came a real live green scaly alligator - all 10 inches of it. The three adults were just amazed that an actual live alligator was in the box. The mailman (who had been carrying this in his mail pouch all day) was so shocked that he passed out and my mother's mother just about joined him in a heap on the porch. Mom's father laughed and laughed. All the while, my mother was so excited that she just danced and sang with joy. Of course, all the neighbors up and down the street stopped doing whatever they were doing and headed over to see the latest addition to 419 Barret Court.

Mother took care of the alligator and it grew and grew and grew and grew until it became about 4 feet long. The alligator lived in the bathtub (the only bathtub in the house). He would be removed from the tub when someone wanted to bathe. However, eventually this became too much and the alligator was banished to the Canton City Zoo where he lived for many more years.

With the exception of the desire to have an exotic pet, my mother had a very usual upbringing for the times. Eventually she would graduate from high school and secretarial school. She got a job working for the local school district and she worked there until she got married and started having children. Eventually after the five of us kids were all enrolled in school, our mother returned to Canton City Schools and she would be employed there until the day she died. (See Chapter Seven – The Deaths). At the time when my mother did go back to work to help support our family, she used it as an opportunity to teach her five children many valuable lessons – how to cook, how to clean, and how to do laundry. All of the chores fell on our shoulders but we were always grateful for the skills we learned as a result.

The greatest thing about my mother was that she was a true mother in every sense of what MOTHER means. She was kind, caring, loving, and concerned that her children accomplish great things with their lives. She was amazing. My mother was the type of woman who never said a bad word about anyone, always made each of us kids feel special and she knew how to stretch limited income to make things good for us kids.

Summer time when we were really young always meant Garage Sales and other cheap entertainment. By careful shopping at garage sales she always stretched the budget to give us extras! My mother and her two friends (Diane & Karen) would load the five of us kids up with the two children of Diane and the three children of Karen in Diane's motor home and off the thirteen of us would go to garage sale after garage sale all over the county. They would always manage to stop at lunch time at a park so that the ten of us kids could get out and run off some energy. Some examples of cheap entertainment were state parks for hikes, a place called

Mother Gooseland (it cost a nickel or a dime per person and you walked around looking at exhibits based on Mother Goose nursery rhymes), bargain matinee movies and basically anything that was advertised as "fun for kids and free". During our travels, I am sure that to the innocent bystander, our entourage looked like a three ring circus but to us it was one exciting adventure after the other.

My mother also taught the five of us the wonders of reading during the summer. She would either take us to the public library or to the Bookmobile so that we could check out books. We were required to check out and read a certain quota, complete with book reports to Mom. Thank goodness she did that because all of us have read books our entire lives because the love of reading mom instilled in each of us. In fact, to this very day those of us who are still living often pass around a book and share it when we find a good one.

The only time my mom put myself and siblings second was when she fell in love with a poodle named Pom-Pom. (As an aside, believe it or not this dog was a male dog & I never understood that name for a boy dog, which possibly could have explained why the dog was such a demon – after all what kind of guy would want to be called POM-POM.) Anyway, this dog was a miniature black poodle that loved my mom and hated myself and my siblings.

From the moment that Satan (I use that name and other variations interchangeably with Pom-Pom), entered our home he terrorized the five of us every chance he got. The dog was like that sneaky little bratty brother or sister that sneaks up on you and bites you and then you scream and as your mom turns to ask what is going on the brat gets that "WHAT? I DIDN'T DO ANYTHING" innocent look on their face and you know that the brat bit you but your mom believes the nasty little liar. At times it felt like my mom loved that dog more than any of us kids – she would put four rubber boots on Devil Dog, a red sweater and a little red cap just to walk the dog outside in bad weather. The evil little dog would prance around almost smirking at me and my siblings. While Pom-Pom lived with us, he always terrorized us whenever possible by chasing us, biting us or destroying our toys. We lived in fear of that evil dog. To prove my point that Pom-Pom was Satan I need to tell you about the day Pom-Pom died and arose from the dead.

It was a beautiful sunny summer day and as I was going out the front door, Pom-Pom pushed past me and ran out of the house and into the road. The demon then managed to get hit by a car. Of course when that happened, my mother rushed out to her beloved poodle (who I just remembered was so messed up he didn't even eat dog food – oh no not Satan's puppy – he had to be fed Cat food but that's a whole different story so let me get back to the death scene . . .) and she knelt down in the middle of the road crying, sobbing and carrying on something horrible. The driver of the car was falling all over herself trying to apologize and comfort my mother. All that my mom could say was "my poor Pom-Pom"!

Meanwhile my mother's five children were gathered at the side of the road (a respectable distance from our grieving mother) and we were high fiving each other and dancing a dance and singing a song about the passing of Satan. It was a total and magnificent (albeit inappropriate) celebration of the end of that dog's tyranny. Our mother managed to ignore our impromptu party. However, I think what we were doing totally freaked out the lady that had hit the dog because I remember hearing her tell our mom – "Mrs. B I think your children are in shock why don't we get you all back into the house." But when my mom wouldn't respond to her request (because Mom was in mourning) and the five of us kept getting louder and more animated in our celebration, the lady literally passed out on the street. Fainted – gone. This only made the five of us laugh more until finally Karen the neighbor came out to help the dog murderer (or in my and my siblings eyes "OUR

LIBERATOR"). It was so surreal but the most bizarre thing was yet to happen, the thing that finally proved that POM-POM was Satan's puppy! Suddenly, the dog's head sort of popped up and he looked around and then he was on his feet shaking his body like a dog does when it is wet and I swear that dog had just risen from the dead for the sole purpose of spiting the five of us kids. Of course what was the first thing he did, he set off chasing the five of us kids. My mother was elated and the five of us kids were deflated in an instant.

I admit the story of that little evil black poodle probably isn't as funny to you my reader as it is to me but if nothing else you can view it as example of just how average my life has always been. If my life was fancy and exotic – old Pom-Pom would have a been a pit bull at least or my mother would have kept a big old grizzly bear as a pet that terrorized her children who with this one exception were the most important things in her life. Instead, the terror of our childhood was just a tiny little poodle.

Having told you now of that weird story of Satan's bow-wow, I will share some additional "odd memories" of my mother (odd only in the fact that I remember these things). I remember that she was always the first one up in the morning & the last one to go to bed at night. Thinking back I can remember not being able to get to sleep on the rare nights that she would go to bed before everyone else – it just wasn't right to go to sleep without hearing her as she watched TV and did all of the last minute chores that she always seemed to be doing. I also remember the rare mornings when I would wake up before she would get up. I can remember lying in bed waiting for her to get up and then I would hear her get up and walk down the hallway. She always had the same type of slippers from sometime in the 1970's. They were a wooden sandal thing – I think they were the product of some Doctor who was an ortho doctor or something – I can't remember the name but anyway as she walked down the hallway to the kitchen those sandals just clipped clopped down the hallway in the same rhythm each and every morning. It was a simple sound but a very reassuring sound. The next morning sound which was repeated every morning was the sound of the refrigerator opening and ice being dumped into a glass and the opening of a can of cola that was then poured into the glass. My mom was addicted to that stuff- she drank it from the time she got up until the time she went to bed. She even kept the syrup to give to us kids when we had stomach aches (and yes it would calm a queasy stomach if served warm). Then after her cola fix, it was time to start my dad's coffee and then the radio would be turned on to listen to the weather (especially during the winter in anticipation of the announcement of snow days) and then one by one she would wake everyone up at the appointed moment so that each person could get in and out of the bathroom and so that we could get off to school or in later years to work. All the while, she would be making breakfast and packing lunches for everyone and tending to every imaginable emergency that can happen in the morning for a family of seven. She was the ultimate multi-tasker each and every morning.

Another odd fact about my mother was how she could move around the house at night while we all slept making sure her children were warm and safely tucked into bed. If she heard a cough in the middle of the night that hadn't been there before bed; she would sneak into that child's bedroom and in the morning, the child that had coughed in his or her sleep would awaken with a greasy menthol rub all over his or her chest. That stuff was strong smelling and just felt nasty. There were mornings when I would wake up and that stuff would be all over my chest and I never remembered coughing during the night nor did I remember her coming in and putting it on me. Mom also was our nurse when we woke up sick in the middle of the night. She would help us back to bed and clean up our messes and then she would go back to bed and still be the first one up in the morning to get the house moving.

Another memory of our mother was that fact that she was never much of a disciplinarian because she always chose to leave that job up to our father. However, it was always quite amusing when one of the five of us kids would push her to her limit. Every time that she got angry enough to yell she would end up going through all five our names just to be able to yell at the child that she wanted to yell at. For example, to yell at me it might come out something like this "CathTruLindKellJay!" Her other favorite thing to say to us when she really was frustrated with or angry with us was to tell us "I hope you each grow up to have five kids just like you are and that they drive you crazy!" The funny part of this was that about two years before she passed away, all five of us kids, spouses and children were at my parent's house swimming and yet again we were driving our mother somewhat crazy with our horsing around. She finally said something about the need for us to calm down and behave like normal people and me being me, I decided to say to her "you just got what you wished for all of your grandchildren act just like their parents and you always said that you hoped that we would grow up and have kids like ourselves." The comment struck a nerve because she just stared at me for a moment and then decided to laugh and just let us be ourselves. One final funny memory about my mother and how the antics of the five of us kids could get on her nerves happened one night when the five of us kids and our mother went to the hospital to visit my father after one of his heart attacks. As we got on the elevator to leave the hospital, four very elderly women also stepped onto the elevator with us. As the elevator doors closed the women all started snipping at each other and they began bantering back and forth. My mother couldn't help herself and she chuckled at them and then she just started laughing. One of the ladies looked at my mother and told her "it's ok sweetie we are sisters and we have been doing this all whole lives – deep down inside we love each other!" My mother without missing a beat said "I wasn't laughing at you for fighting, I was laughing because I saw the future of these five kids because they sound just like you and they always have and they will still be doing it when they are old and gray."

When we weren't driving my mother crazy, she was always playing cheerleader and motivator to push us to be our best. In my case, my mother was my biggest supporter and the main reason why I was able to graduate from college. She pushed me to do it and helped me succeed. When I was gone during Operation Desert Storm during 1990 & 1991 with my Army Reserve Unit, she spent so many sleepless nights it was a wonder she was able to function. (See Chapter Five – War). She watched nothing on TV except a 24 hour news channel and she was always worried for the seven months that I was gone. She even had a TV on her desk at work (with her boss' permission). She organized friends and family to write to me – making sure that I received at least one letter each and every day that I was gone. She involved herself in the family support group that was started for my reserve unit and she helped raise money for that group. She worried day in and day out. I often thought that this was silly and I tried to tell her to stop worrying but she never did until I was back in the house. It wouldn't be until 2005 when my nephew went to Iraq with the United States Marines that I would understand why she worried. She worried because of the unknown. I know this because it was the exact same thing that caused me to worry in 2005 for my nephew's safety and it was then that I finally was able to truly appreciate the love that my mom had for me.

The greatest gift that my mom gave to me was an example to try and live up to. I don't know if I have ever reached that level yet but I have always tried to live up to her standards in all the decisions that I have made.

FATHER

My father on the other hand was the complete opposite of my mother in so many ways. I have often wondered how they ever met and how they ever fell in love. My father was seven years older than my mother and had a completely different upbringing than my mother and lived a completely different life than my mother. Yet they did meet and they fell in love and because of that I was born.

I really don't have a cute story about my father like my mother's alligator story. However, there were a lot of stories of things like dropping out of school, smoking from the time he was fourteen onward, and racing cars as a young man – all the things that if any of his five children would have done, he would have killed us.

One of the few funny stories that I can remember about my father involves bottle rockets and the Fourth of July about 1979. My father had rigged up this metal pipe/launch tube so that he could sit in his lawn chair just inside the garage and shoot off his bottle rockets (which were illegal in Ohio at the time) and drink his beer. On that fourth, there in the garage sat my entire family as we watched him shoot off his bottle rockets when all of a sudden one sort of misfired and barely lifted off the ground. Just as it failed to launch a sheriff's deputy was driving down the street. The bottle rocket actually skimmed across the hood of the car and died when it was in the center of the car hood. There it exploded. The deputy of course stopped his car and turned on his flashing lights. My father was busted. His reaction was that he quickly grabbed his stash of bottle rockets and his launch tube and he threw them under my mother's car in the garage. Clank, clank, clank went his metal bottle rocket launch tube as it rolled to the other end of the garage. As the deputy got out of his car and started walking up the driveway, my mother just kept saying "you are in trouble now, I told you not to shoot those things, you are in trouble now." My dad looked very guilty and very scared. As the deputy walked up the driveway, he looked at my dad and said "Don!"

Luckily for my dad the deputy was an old friend of his and my father got off with a wink and a nod of a warning. After the deputy left he just sat there saying "I was never scared – I knew I could get out of it!" My brother and sisters and I just laughed because we knew he was just acting big because for just a few moments (as he threw his rocket launching tube) he truly thought he was in big time trouble.

My father was a carpenter and worked construction most of his life and as a result he definitely had very colorful language. The worst thing about his language was his use of the "N" word in describing African Americans. I look back now and I am amazed at the racist things that he would say. These comments sounded normal growing up but eventually I would learn just how horrible they were. I don't excuse the things he would say but over the years I grew to understand where the comments came from. I am just glad to say that in later years before he died he actually changed his beliefs on this subject. (See Chapter "Deaths")

The one thing that you could definitely say about my father is the fact that he ruled the roost at home – it was his way or no way. If the five of us kids misbehaved for our mom all she had to say was "wait till your father gets home" and we settled down instantly. Also if we were bad when he was home, my father only had to start undoing his big brown belt because we knew we didn't want the belt. If my father was raising his children in the 1990s or later as opposed to the 1960s and 1970s he would have been in prison for child abuse. I am sure I agree with the modern theory of "spare the rod" but I can tell you this about my father's child rearing thoughts - my siblings who have children didn't grow up to be child abusers because of his corporal punishment and the lessons learned about right from wrong served us well in so much as none of us were ever incarcerated as criminals. We turned out ok but I do think there were times he went too far but we survived and we all became productive members of society. I even became President of the United States of America.

Most of the time, if someone would have asked me about my dad's discipline, I would have said some very unflattering things about him and his methods. However, there were moments when it was pretty funny! Let's see there was the threat – "I am going to beat your butt till it bleeds buttermilk!" The five of us kids always laughed about that one. Then of course there were the many many times that we would all be in the car heading somewhere and the five of us kids would be fighting and picking on each other and he would be driving down the road at 70 – 80 mph while he was trying to reach into the backseat to swat us kids. It is a wonder that we are still alive but it was great fun to watch that hand reach back to try and hit us and we always were able to dodge that reach (since none of us had on seatbelts).

Of all the things to remember about my father, I remember beer and cigarettes. This was a man who the first thing he did in the morning and the last thing he did at night before climbing into bed was smoke a cigarette. He would also pop the top on a beer at 10:00am in the morning on the weekends (after work on workdays) and continue drinking until bedtime. Now the beer back in those days was bought in cardboard cases in bottles that had to be returned when you bought the next case – they were not disposable bottles. My father kept his case of beer downstairs in the basement of our house in the room we called the well pit. The well pit for those of you that don't know was a room under the front porch outside of the walls of the basement that housed the well that supplied our home with water. It was always the same cool temperature in there – winter, spring, summer or fall. So the beer according to my father was the right temperature all the time. The worst part of this was that when he wanted a beer after a long hard day of work, he sent one of us kids down to get the beer. Plus, we had to return the previous empty bottle stinking of that stale beer smell to put back into the cardboard case to be returned when the entire 24 bottles were empty. In my case, having to go down to the basement was one of my worst nightmares come to life. I hated the basement and I feared all of the monsters that lived in the basement. So every time I had to go get a beer, I lived in fear. Yes, I know that was very wimpy but that was a part of my childhood.

In regards to the cigarettes, my father was so addicted to the nicotine that the first time he had Congestive Heart Failure in the late eighties; I awoke to hear him and my mom out the front porch arguing over whether or not that would be the best time for him to have a cigarette or not.

My father was gasping for air and saying "JUST . . . LET ME (GASP) . . . SMOKE A CIGARETTE (GASP GASP) – IT … WILL HELP ME . . . (GASP) CATCH MY BREATH!" There he was dying and he was thinking that a cigarette could give him a breathing treatment. So I got up went to the phone and called 911 and had the ambulance come to the house. He was so furious at me but I just kept thinking "my God the man is dying and he is going to use his last breath to suck on a cigarette". After several more episodes of Congestive Heart Failure, my father would suffer a massive heart attack in Iowa while on vacation with my mother. It was so bad that my siblings and I were called to go to Iowa and be with him because the doctor didn't think he would make it (in fact the doctor didn't even think that our dad would survive until we got to Iowa from Ohio). However, he did end up surviving and when my siblings needed to return to Ohio to return to work, I (since I had a flexible work schedule) was the lucky one that was left in Iowa to drive my parents back home in his van.

The day we checked him out of the hospital was typical of my father. The man was on oxygen and even though the doctor had wanted him to fly home and not drive for 12 hours, there we were in the van driving home because my father refused to fly. He knew better than the medical doctor who had just saved his life. To make the situation even more stressful, the Missippi River was expected to reach flood stage levels within hours after the time we were to be crossing it. When we left, we were on a strict time schedule to get across the river before they closed the flood gates.

The first thing he demanded when we got into the van was the keys so that he could drive his van home. So yet again my father and I argued because I wouldn't give him the keys. His argument was that it was his van and he had never given me permission to drive it to Iowa and since it was his van he would be the one to drive it home. He lost the argument because I simply wouldn't give up the keys and he wasn't strong enough due to the heart attack to do a damn thing about it. Then after the argument, he tells me to find a store and get him a pack of cigarettes.

I just looked at the man and said "are you out of your mind?" I tried to explain to him that oxygen and flames didn't mix and that I didn't want to die in an explosion on the interstate. However, I was informed that he knew that fact and that he wouldn't cause an explosion because he knew what he was doing. I never stopped at a store but rather I found the interstate and headed home. When we did stop to get gas, he was too weak to walk into the store on the journey home and he never got the cigarettes. However, I think he was angry with me about that trip home until his dying day. I mean how did I dare to drive his van to Iowa to get him to bring him home and just how could I not allow him to drive after a massive heart attack and finally just how could I refuse him a cigarette while he was on oxygen. I mean clearly I was a horrible son.

The trip home from Iowa was not the first time we ever argued. Growing up I don't remember my father and I agreeing on anything. If I said something was white he would say it was black. I would talk about things that I learned at school and it would always lead to an argument. I could never figure this out. It was as if he had no use for school. In fact whenever I said that I wanted to grow up and go to college, his usual answer was that college would be a waste of time and that he wasn't about to pay to send me to college. Instead he believed that I should go to the military and that the military would make a man out of me. My standard answer was that I was never going to join the military and we would argue some more. (Never say Never)

My relationship with my father was a lot like two cars going down a one way street but in different directions. Yep – a head on collision. As a result, I never thought that my father was happy with me and I was never happy with him for the most part. I also certainly never thought that he was proud of me. At various times, as a child and a young man, I believed that he actually hated me. There were many times when I just didn't want to be around him. I only figured out our relationship after he died.

Part of our problem was that we both inherited a very Stubborn Gene from his father – Grandpa Charlie and that gene means that no matter what I am right and you are wrong about any and all subjects. Let's just say it made for some interesting dinners at our house. The old man's stubbornness and my stubbornness also made for some interesting punishments when I would make my dad angry. Our eternal struggle during punishment time was especially apparent when I was a young boy. My dad loved to make the five of us stand in the corner as a punishment until we apologized and admitted our wrong doing. More often than not, when he punished me in this manner, it became an epic battle of wills with me usually winning because I had this talent of being able to fall asleep standing up in the corner. This of course just made him angrier and so he would wake me up and then I would go right back to sleep. Usually I won in so much as he would give up and just send me off to bed.

Our polar oppositeness also meant that I never managed to learn all the carpentry things that my father could have taught me. My father like his father was an outstanding carpenter. However, I didn't want to take the time to learn anything that my father had to teach me and my father couldn't teach me in a manner that would allow me to learn. His idea of teaching was that I was to stand there and watch him do whatever task he was doing and absorb what he was doing by osmosis. I was just suppose to hand him the tools that he needed and clean up after him. The biggest flaw in his plan was that because he had never actually taught me these things, I had no idea what tool he wanted me to hand him let alone be able to hand him the right tool when he wanted it which would just make him angry. I just wish we could have found some common ground so that I could have learned just a small amount of knowledge from him. However, I didn't and that is old news.

Just like he wasn't big on teaching me by normal means, my father wasn't big on using father and son talks to teach about life. The closest my father ever came to actually giving the five of us kids any advice was the fact that he always told the five us to never get arrested because if we did he would leave us in jail. There was never discussions about career choices, no sex talks, no talks about finances – just the "don't get arrested because you are going to stay in jail" talk. That was my dad.

In fact crime played an important role in one of the most memorable stories that I have of my father when I was growing up. Two houses up from my family's home was the home of an older gentleman who had three Plum trees. Those trees had the sweetest and juiciest plums in the world. Mr. Sourston's only rule as it related to the plums was that the neighborhood kids could eat whatever we wanted from the ones that dropped on the ground.

However, we were not allowed to pick any plums from the tree. For years, we never violated that rule.

Then one summer Mr. Sourston was down in South Carolina visiting his daughter about the time those plums ripened. We, the neighborhood kids, had devoured all the plums that had fallen to the ground. However, like the serpent and that certain tree in the Bible we were tempted and we were weak. Suddenly, almost like we had no control over our bodies, we climbed those trees on auto pilot just to eat the forbidden fruit. Kid after kid climbed the trees picking one, picking two, picking three plums and suddenly all three trees were picked clean and there we sat underneath the trees feasting when Mr. Sourston came driving into his driveway. It was like he knew we would be there and we would be eating those plums. He gave chase but we got away – after all how was a 90 year old man who walked with a cane going to catch a group of kids all under the age of 14. So by escaping, we thought that we had gotten away with the great plum caper but of course we hadn't. That night as each father came home from work, Mr. Sourston made his rounds. Most of the other kids denied that they had been there and that they had stolen any plums but this was the 70s and parents believed other adults. That night on Gephart street there wasn't a single kid who wasn't yelled and screamed at by his or her father with the exception of the Barton Five.

Surprisingly, our father, who was always a screamer or a belt whipping father, remained extremely calm. He called each of us into the living room and asked us "did you steal the plums?" We knew better than to lie and we admitted our guilt and to our surprise and utter astonishment, he never yelled. One by one he asked and one by one he dismissed us after our answer. As a group we were shocked. We were amazed to hear the yelling up and down the street and nothing from our father. He never said a word during dinner. However, when dinner was over he dropped the hammer of death. As was his custom on Friday night, he yelled "Allowance Time" and five eager children came running with hands out ready to be paid the money that we already knew how we were going to spend. He handed each of us our allowances and then just as we thought that we had escaped his wrath over the plums plus gotten paid he calmly said "line up – oldest to youngest."

He then marched us straight out the front door, down the sidewalk, down the driveway and up the road to Mr. Sourston's house. He marched us with the precision of a Marine Drill Sergeant. Then he ordered us one by one to walk up to the door, to knock, to say "I am a thief" and "please accept my apology". Then we were instructed to hand over our allowance in restitution. Finally, he marched us back down the street to our own home. He went into the house and never said another word about the plums. My siblings and I were humiliated and embarrassed. However, the lesson had been learned and to my knowledge to this day not a one of us has ever stolen or even thought of stealing anything again.

Ultimately, the gift that I credit my father with giving to me is the knowledge that nothing in life is free – you have to put a lot of hard work into all things in life in order to reap the rewards.

GRANDPA CHARLIE vs GRANDFATHER LEEPER

The next two ancestors I wish to discuss are my grandfathers who like my father and mother were polar opposites. As much as Grandpa Charlie (my dad's dad) was an ordinary average man who could be crude, my Grandfather Leeper was dignified and refined. Grandpa Charlie was short & thin while Grandfather Leeper was tall and on the heavy side. Grandpa Charlie never made it past the 8th grade and Grandfather Leeper was a college graduate. Over the years before he died Grandpa Charlie used some pretty rough language whereas I don't think I ever heard Grandfather Leeper say a bad word. Grandpa Charlie was also a bigot when it came to race issues and he wasn't afraid to use the "N" word. This he passed down to my father and my father passed it onto me (at least onto me until I turned 17 and joined the Army which I will be getting to later). Grandfather Leeper on the other hand respected all men who earned his respect by their actions and not their skin colors.

Grandpa Charlie would tell stories about all the many different jobs he had once held (Carpenter, Farmer, Streetcar Conductor, Blacksmith, Plumber, Electrician, and Factory worker to name just a few) vs the fact that Grandfather Leeper was an engineer with the electric company for his entire working career. During World War II, Grandfather Leeper and his family stayed in Canton, Ohio. At the same time, Grandpa Charlie packed up his entire family and they traveled all over the country towing a camping trailer behind them to live in as they worked construction job after construction job for the defense plants being built for the War effort.

As much as they were different both of these men shared one really cool characteristic – their sense of humor. I remember one time at Christmas, Grandpa Charlie was making gifts for my mom, and my two aunts. The gifts were these miniature fireplaces. The fireplaces were made to resemble a fireplace from an old log cabin. He had no plans to work off of but rather he was creating these little miniatures from his head. He carved and manufactured every single item on the fireplaces. They had hearths, fires, the fireplace tools, cooking pots and pans, mantles with tiny pictures hanging over them and even a musket hanging over the mantle. They were incredible pieces of folk art when you consider he made each and every piece himself and they looked so real. This man thought of every little detail including a bearskin rug in front of the fireplace. I was amazed and when I asked him about the bearskin rugs he got his sly, "cat who ate the canary" smile on his face and he said I'll tell you but you can't tell anyone else. So he told me that he had been catching mice and skinning them to make the bearskin rugs. I was shocked and said no way! But then he showed me the last mouse that he had just caught and right there before me he skinned the mouse and had a perfect little rug for the fireplace that he was making. I must have been standing there with my mouth wide open because he started laughing like he had just heard or seen the funniest thing ever. Then two weeks later on Christmas morning my mom opened up her gift from Grandpa Charlie (as did my two aunts) and everyone was just oohing and ahhing over the works of art that he had created. My mom asked "what did you make the rug out of? It looks like real fur" and my grandpa just kind of chuckled and said something about it being a secret. Well, I was kind of ornry as a kid and I chimed in "I know what it is!" Everyone looked at me expecting me to tell all since Grandpa Charlie wouldn't. So without thinking I shouted out that they were Mouse Pelts and that I had seen Grandpa Charlie skin one of them. Everyone sat there and laughed and my mom told everyone to ignore me because according to her, I tended to exaggerate at times. I screamed "no sir it was true they were mouse pelts" and everyone looked at Grandpa Charlie. He with a very straight face looked at everyone in that room and said that they weren't mouse pelts but that he had told me to say that just to get everyone laughing. Immediately everyone started laughing and as I looked at Grandpa Charlie he winked at me and he had that sly, "cat that ate the canary" grin back on his face. Later that day he whispered in my ear that they were mice but that if anyone knew that they were then my mom and my aunts wouldn't want them so it would just have to be our little secret. To this day, I laugh about my mom and my two aunts displaying those mice pelts in their living rooms for the entire world to see. Thanks Grandpa Charlie for the laugh! Grandfather Leeper had a great sense of humor too. He loved to tell jokes and even when they weren't all that funny he would start to laugh and soon everyone in the room would be laughing. His laugh was the best and I can't really describe it but it was one of those distinctive laughs that just felt good to hear. I can't really remember any one particular funny incident with him like the

Mouse Pelts from Grandpa Charlie but his stories were hilarious like when he would tell the story about my mom and her alligator or he would tell stories about his early years growing up on a farm in rural southern Ohio.

Both of these men remain to this day important parts of me because they made me an important part of their lives. I was important to Grandpa Charlie because even though I wasn't his first Grandson, I was his first "BARTON" grandson. I was his hope to carry on the name. Grandpa Charlie was sure that I would carry on his family name and do it with pride and honor. (Ironically, even though I became President of the USA, I feel as though I let him down. As is typical in my life I didn't do what was expected of me so I never had any children let alone a son to carry on the BARTON name, so my Grandpa Charlie should have spent more time with my brother who actually carried on the Barton name with 6 sons of his own) I still remember the stories he made me memorize about my Barton ancestors. He was proud of his family history even if it wasn't the most noteworthy of families. Our family history was one of hard working average Americans. He always told me that as long as I was honest and worked hard, I would be a success. Material riches didn't make a man a success but being able to know that your name was good and stood for something positive was the greatest measure of success. Of course, he would tell me this as he told me stories of shooting at the African Americans (truthfully he used the "N" word not African Americans) who would try to get on the streetcar when he was the conductor. Luckily, I learned the true lesson that going through life without disgracing your family name was a good thing even if Grandpa Charlie thought that the family name only had to be respected in the white world.

Like Grandpa Charlie, Grandfather Leeper was thrilled to have a grandson. My three older sisters were ok as grandchildren but a grandson was very important to my grandfather. He had been the first Leeper grandson and his grandfather my great great grandfather Leeper had made a huge deal out of him so I guess he thought that was the right thing to do. Anyway, Grandfather Leeper spent hours and hours with me taking me here and there doing the Grandfather/Grandson thing! For me it was great fun. He would take me around to his barber to meet all of his old cronies and they would share stories. The funny thing is when we would leave, the barber would always ask me "son what are you going to do with your life when you grow up and become a man?" and before I could answer, Grandfather Leeper would say "he is going to be a great man in fact he will make a great President of the United States of America someday" and out the door we would go. In my mind, I would laugh because I never really thought that would happen but yet it did in the year 2016.

The gift that my grandfathers each gave to me was a sense of pride in who I am and who came before me and the importance of a good name. Oh yeah and a sense of humor is a great thing too!

Great Aunt Ruth

Let me start this out by saying that no matter what I write about this lady it won't be enough because she was such a character. I actually think I should be writing an entire book about this lady and only this lady. Everyone on the planet Earth should have a Great Aunt Ruth.

Great Aunt Ruth was a retired school teacher from a one room school house in Southern Ohio. She divorced her husband in a time when divorce carried a huge stigma let alone the stigma of a woman divorcing her husband. She was a take charge woman who lived her life on her own terms and only her terms.

One of her favorite stories from the days when she taught school was about the School Superintendent's son. It seems that the young man would blow a whistle every time Great Aunt Ruth had her back to the class. This went on for several days and she couldn't figure out which student was blowing the whistle. One day when she was in the back of the classroom, the young man mistakenly thought she was outside and he blew the whistle. Well, now she had the guilty party so she marched up the aisle grabbed him and pulled him out of his seat and walked him to the front of the room. She took the whistle and grabbed her paddle. As she prepared to paddle this child she asked him whether or not he had anything to say for himself. Well this young man looked her straight in the eyes and said "you can't paddle me – my father is the Superintendent of the schools and he will fire you if you paddle me." Great Aunt Ruth just looked at him for a shocked moment and then she bent him over and smacked the child's butt. As she prepared to swing again and as the child stood crying like a little girl, the School Superintendent walked into the schoolhouse. He demanded to know what she thought she was doing to his son. My Great Aunt Ruth looked at the man and said "this is my classroom and I am disciplining a juvenile delinquent just like I punished his father when his father misbehaved in my classroom." Well this of course embarrassed the superintendent and he ordered her to stop. She looked him straight in the eye and said "this is my classroom, I mete out punishment and this child is going to be spanked. If you wish to get in my way, I will whip you right along with him. If you don't want that to happen, I suggest you leave now and allow me to finish what I started." Instantly, the Superintendent turned and left because he knew Great Aunt Ruth and he knew she would do it.

When I was born she was already 88 years old. She would live to be 110 and she was as sharp as could be until the day that she died. How exactly she lived to be 110 is one of those great mysteries in life. This woman up until when she came to live with my family

(As a side note: She would only consent to live with us during the winter months and at times the five of us were very grateful to see her return to her own house for the summers so that we could regain our freedom to run wild without direct supervision.) at the age of 98 had never lived in a home with indoor plumbing. At the age of 98 she was still pumping her water from a hand pump in the backyard. She was still walking out to the outhouse when nature called. In addition, she lived in a house that had limited electricity but no phone, no television, no central heat, and no refrigerator. Her diet consisted of stewed tomatoes, prunes, coffee (which she didn't drink but rather put it in a saucer over crushed up saltine crackers and ate it like soup), bread, butter, coleslaw, meat (whatever she would go and buy at the grocery store each day since she didn't have a refrigerator) and one box of wafer cookies per day. Yes one entire box of wafer cookies per day. Yet she was as skinny as could be. She was tall and had absolutely white hair with exception of one streak of red from her youth.

Perhaps her secret to longevity was her cure all which was the original Listerine. No matter what ailed her, it was Listerine to the rescue. (Please note I don't think you are supposed to swallow Listerine so please read the warning label before trying Great Aunt Ruth's cure). Upset stomach take a swig of Listerine. Headache – another swig of Listerine. Sore throat – yep Listerine. The worst thing that she did with Listerine was that she used it when she got a cut because that meant she would open the bottle and pour it over the cut which had to burn like hell!! Every time, I ever saw her pour it on a cut I would cringe. Even now while writing this so many years later, I am cringing thinking of how much it had to have burnt.

When Great Aunt Ruth came to live with us we also got another boarder – sort of a two for one special. She came with her very own pet – one named CANEY. Yes a walking cane that she had named Caney. She would talk to Caney and even call out for

Caney to come to her. This of course was quite humorous to the five Barton Heathens.

We kids also took great amusement in her wonderment of television. She had never had it in her home but she loved to watch it once she moved in. The only problem was she developed a fondness for programs the five of us didn't care for but were forced to watch because of her. This of course was back in the days when we only received three channels, had no remote controls, no vcrs, no dvrs, and only had one TV in the entire house. However, eventually we came to enjoy the shows as much as she did or perhaps we just enjoyed watching her watch TV. She loved to watch a show that used to be on called Joker's Wild. I really don't remember the show or the concept only that the contestant would pull a lever like on a Slot Machine in Vegas and the wheels would spin around and every once in awhile a Joker would pop up. I don't remember if the Joker was a good thing or bad thing for the contestant but Great Aunt Ruth would get such delight out of it. Her other favorite program was Hee Haw – I don't have to say anything else about that if you have ever seen it. If you haven't seen it, look it up on the internet – I am sure you will be amused. The five of us kids were also amused when the reception wasn't working on the TV and it would look like the screen was full of snow (those who have never had old style television won't understand that) Great Aunt Ruth actually thought it was real snow and she would say she hoped that it would stop snowing so she could watch her programs.

When Great Aunt Ruth came to live with us not only did she change our TV viewing schedule but she also totally upset the routine in the house for us kids. Our mother was a working mother by that time and therefore, we were accustomed to coming home from school and somewhat running wild and free. We had chores to do that our mother had assigned and we were held accountable to accomplishing those chores but basically as long as they were done we did whatever the heck we wanted. Not so once the retired teacher entered into our lives. We were forced to come home from school, report to her what our assigned chore was and report to her what homework we had. She then allowed us time to do the chores and then made us do our homework. Homework wasn't complete until she had graded it (try explaining to your teacher why your homework was pre-graded when you turned it in the next day) and we had corrected our errors. In addition, we were subject to her quizzes based on the previous days work. When and if she was satisfied we were let out of school and allowed to play. Very rarely was this before my mother returned home from work.

Not only did she feel that she had to earn her keep by being babysitter and teacher after school, Great Aunt Ruth felt that she had to earn her keep by drying the dishes. At that point in time the five of us kids each had one night that we had to wash dishes and it was child abuse washing dishes with Great Aunt Ruth drying dishes. When we handed off the washed dish it had to be scalding hot or she wouldn't dry it and she would drop it back into the soapsuds to be washed again. As a result our hands became immune to hot water (to the point where each of us could actually reach into a pot of boiling water and pull something out of the pot with no injury). Just kidding actually we all learned a very useful trick. We kept the temperature in the soapy water at a comfortable level and then left the hot water running on her side of the sink and after we washed the dish we carefully ran it under the hot water right before we handed it off to her. More often than not we would run out of hot water in the hot water tank as a result of leaving the water running. In addition, by leaving the water running we weren't doing a very good job for the environment but it was back before everyone was trying to be "GREEN" and politically correct.

Two very odd facts stick out in my mind about Great Aunt Ruth and they both centered on her two greatest fears about death. The first one was the fact that at the age of 99 she still had most of her own teeth even if they were in terrible shape. She was afraid to die with her natural teeth in the state that they were for fear that they would look horrible while she laid in her casket and people viewed her body. So at the age of 99 Great Aunt Ruth decided she needed a beautiful new set of false teeth. However, at the time she wasn't the most "mobile" person in the world and my mother wasn't sure she could get her into and out of a dentist office. Eventually, Mother found a dentist with an office that was relatively easy for her to get Great Aunt Ruth in and out of (along with the assistance of my father, a couple of my sisters and probably several of the dentist's office staff). So my mom made the appointments, Great Aunt Ruth was hauled into the office and the teeth were pulled. The problem was that the dentist who pulled the teeth didn't make false teeth.

So my mom being the giving person that she was she started checking around and eventually she found a dentist who would come to the house and do what he needed to do to make the teeth (impressions & fittings) right there in our kitchen. So after the pulling of the teeth ordeal and the somewhat comic impressions and fittings being done in my mother's kitchen in front of an audience of the Barton Five and weeks of waiting Aunt Ruth ended up with a beautiful set of Pearly Whites. True to her word like always the teeth were for her to wear in her casket so after she got them she stashed them away in a dresser drawer. Then for the last 11 years of her life she never wore them – nope she kept them stored away in a velvet bag and she made my mother swear that she would have them in Great Aunt Ruth's mouth when she laid in her casket. Now this sort of led to a problem. Since she had no teeth for 11 years her mouth kind of sunk in and shrunk and we all got used to seeing her with no teeth. So when she passed away and she got to the funeral home the mortician had a terrible time getting the teeth into her shrunken mouth and as a result there she lay in her casket with a full set of teeth which we were not used to and to be blunt, she kind of had this grotesque eerie smile on her face. Think of the Joker's smile in Batman and then think even stranger! In addition, because she had outlived all of her friends, by the time she died the only people at her funeral were my parents, I, my siblings and about 5 of our relatives on my dad's side of the family (who were there out of obligation). So, since all of us had seen her without the teeth, she never really needed the death teeth but she had the teeth in death.

The second odd thing about Aunt Ruth and death was the fact that she had purchased her headstone for her cemetery lot back in the 1950s and it was pre lettered with her name and year of birth (1877) and then they added the 19 thinking that they would only have to add the last two digits when she died. However, when 1985 rolled around and she was still alive and well, she started to worry and fret about that headstone. What would happen if she lived 15 more years? How would they ever get the 19 off and put 20 on there? This was all she worried about for 1985, 1986, and the portion of 1987 that she lived. There is a part of me that believes that some of the worry led to her demise at the age of 110 in 1987. She just couldn't get over the fear of making it to 2000.

Now I know that what I have written probably seems a little irreverent about Great Aunt Ruth but in reality, I can say I truly loved the woman and greatly respected her. She was tough and fair and she taught me so many things. She was the perfect example of the wisdom that the elderly have to share and are willing to share with younger generations. She actually gave me two wonderful gifts! The first gift was the lesson that with age comes wisdom. The second gift was that by respecting that wisdom and listening to one's elders, I could learn all of the important lessons in life (However, as I stated earlier the exception to this rule was that I didn't think I could learn anything from my father).

Uncle Bruce & Aunt Doreen

Uncle Bruce was my mother's brother and I received my middle name from him. Actually a true and interesting story about the name was the fact that my maternal grandparents used to read books and magazine stories written by one Bruce Barton. Since, they enjoyed his books they decided to name their son Bruce after their favorite author. Then later my mother grew up and married a man with the last name of Barton. When my parents started having children they decided to name each of their children with family names. So when I was born my mother thought that it would be a great idea that I would become Bruce Barton. The Jay was added to give me my own distinct name and so that I wouldn't have to share it with the author. (Two side notes about when I was named follow: First my mother briefly thought about naming me after her father's deceased brother and my father's dad which would have made me Ray Charles. Second, was the fact that my mom had this thing going on where she named all of her children with a name that ended in Y and which provided my older sisters yet another means to torture me with while we were growing up. You see my mother named my sisters Cathy, Trudy, Lindy and my brother was named Kelly. So my siblings loved to tell me that I was adopted because even though my name ended in a Y it was different because Cathee, Lindee, Trudee and Kellee's names all had the long E sound. Jay does not unless I wanted to be called Jayee.)

Anyway, getting back to Uncle Bruce & Aunt Doreen and their part of my story; I have to say Uncle Bruce and Aunt Doreen were the closest relatives that I had that were rich and worldly unlike the rest of us simple folks from Ohio. Uncle Bruce had gone into the Army at the very end of WW II and never saw any action (which is a good thing). For the duration of his military service, Uncle Bruce was stationed as a radio operator in Alaska. After he got out he used his military benefits to go to college and he earned a degree in Engineering. He then put his degree to work going around the world building huge draglines for the Coal Industry.

On one of his trips he met my Aunt Doreen in England in a small coal mining town. She and her family owned the inn where he stayed. They fell instantly in love and had a wonderful time and right before he was to leave, he proposed marriage. She just wasn't sure and said "No". After he left Doreen was miserable and in her heartbreak, she wrote him everyday. She regretted not accepting his marriage proposal as soon as he was gone. She prayed and prayed and prayed that he would return to England and she made herself a promise that she would never let him go if he did. Then one night there was an accident at the coal mine where his giant dragline had been built – a solid steel beam snapped in two destroying the dragline. The break in the steel and the way that it broke was a mystery. In fact to this day the mystery has never been solved by any expert anywhere. The only explanation according to Aunt Doreen was LOVE. She loved Uncle Bruce so much and wanted him to return to England but he couldn't because of work so the steel beam had to break to make him return to her. That time she married him and didn't let him leave without her.

From that moment on they lived a wonderful life together. They traveled to exotic lands all over the world on his engineering projects. They would bring back great gifts for me and my siblings with great stories. We always would talk about Uncle Bruce and Aunt Doreen with a certain air of awe and respect. It was also fun to brag to our friends and neighbors about the fact that Uncle Bruce was in Hong Kong or Saudi Arabia or Morocco or anyplace else (not that we knew where some of these places were when we were real young) but they sounded so much better than Louisville, Ohio or even Canton, Ohio.

Eventually Uncle Bruce would end up working for NASA down at Cape Canaveral on the Apollo Missions to the Moon. He worked down there for about 3 years nonstop. His work was classified and he really couldn't talk about any of it. (One of the first things I did when I took office as President of the United States was to look at his classified projects – I was proud as a child but even more proud of his successes when as I sat in the Oval Office and I learned all the details of what he had accomplished). While he worked for NASA on the actual projects, Aunt Doreen worked for NASA in Hospitality, since, she and her family had run a hotel in England and she had formal training in hospitality. Plus it didn't hurt that she knew how to throw a really good party. So that is what she did for NASA. Whenever there were members of Congress or other VIPs in Florida to check up on Apollo, my Aunt was the one to throw the parties. She had so much fun and she was very good at the job. She used to love to tell my mom that she had met this person and that person. They would discuss what the women wore, how handsome the men were and all that normal gossip. Years later I was amazed to be sitting at her dining room table in England looking through scrapbooks with her and seeing all the pictures of Aunt Doreen and Uncle Bruce with congressmen, the President of the United States (Johnson and Nixon), the Queen of England and a whole host of celebrities.

The sad part about Uncle Bruce was that just a few years after the United States landed on the moon; he passed away from a massive heart attack. He suffered the heart attack while on assignment in Saudi Arabia and it was quite the ordeal getting him home to Ohio for his funeral. His funeral was actually the first funeral that I really remember in my life. I remember the calling hours and the service and the sadness. It was the first time in my life that I understood that when a person dies then he would be gone forever. It was at his funeral, that I learned that funerals were an end to life as we know it.

The worst part of his funeral that I remember is the drive to the cemetery. The cemetery where he was laid to rest was an hour and a half away from Canton and while we were driving down the expressway the driver of the hearse fell asleep. The hearse went across the two southbound lanes, crossed over the median strip and went into the northbound lanes while heading south. Not only did the hearse almost rollover while crossing the median it was almost in several head on collisions before the driver woke up. Terror and Sadness are not a great combination for a nine year old child. To this day when I think of that hearse weaving across the different lanes of the highway, I get sick to my stomach.

After the funeral, Aunt Doreen decided to stay in the United States but eventually her grief forced her to return to her family in England. However, she would return to the States annually to check on her American nieces and nephews and her arrival was always eagerly awaited with excitement that we would get to see her and the excitement of knowing that we would get to go to the Train station in the middle of the night. You see Aunt Doreen didn't like to fly so she would come to New York, New York by cruise ship and then from NY to Ohio via the train.

Since the train station was in a very bad section of town there was always an element of danger to the trip and of course that just thrilled the Barton Five. I was always surprised that my parents would load us up in the car in the middle of the night and take off for the station to pick up Aunt Doreen. I remember my parents would whisper about the fact that the train station was where hoods hung out to sell drugs and that prostitutes hung out at the station too. At the time, I didn't know what a hood was nor did I know what a prostitute was but with my active imagination, I couldn't wait to see them. On one of our trips, as we stood in the station waiting for the train to arrive a young lady approached a man standing close to my father. The lady was dressed in a very short skirt and she was a wearing a ton of makeup. She asked the man if he wanted "a date". At that point, my mother kind of shuffled the five of us kids a little further down the platform away from the lady looking for a date. Suddenly, it dawned on me that since my mother was nervous this lady must be one of the whispered about hoods or prostitutes. So, I, being the inquisitive lad that I was, I shouted out to my mother "is that lady a hood or a prostitute?" My mother froze (as did every other adult on that platform) for a moment and then she grabbed the five of us kids and herded us off to the car. Once inside the car, I was given a stern lecture complete with a definition of a prostitute by mother. According to my mother a prostitute was a bad lady who wore a lot of makeup and inappropriate clothing. Just a couple years after that as a teenager, I found out that my mother was a little off in her definition. Luckily, Aunt Doreen's train arrived and once she got into the car, the lecture ended.

Sometimes, because of my overactive imagination, I would wonder why my parents would take us out to that neighborhood so late at night. The cynic in me would start to think that perhaps they thought nobody would attack people if children were in the car. It was either that or my mom & dad thought they could throw the hoodlums a couple of children to buy themselves some time to get away. Luckily, we never found out because in spite of the scary people that were always hanging out at the train station our family was never harmed or bothered waiting on the Lady from England.

Aunt Doreen's visits also meant that the five of us kids didn't have to go to school the next day and we got to brag that our Aunt from England was visiting us. We loved to see her and visit with her. I remember something about her that is kind of an odd memory but it seems I always have odd memories. My siblings and I thought at the time that it was very cool to watch her smoke and blow smoke rings into the air. We also loved her visits because we were also your typical greedy children so we loved to see what she had brought us from England. Another great part was that while she visited, we would get to go out to eat a lot (back in the 70s families didn't eat out in restaurants very often and when there were seven members in a family it was even less!) Two great stories come to mind about going out to dinner with Aunt Doreen. For the first story you have to be able to remember the 1970's when fast food restaurants would serve hamburgers in Styrofoam containers. We had stopped at one of those places when we went down to visit Uncle Bruce's grave with Aunt Doreen. The place would serve the hamburgers plain but they had a bar set up where the patrons could add lettuce, onions, pickles etc to their hamburgers. Well when Aunt Doreen saw the nice little container that her hamburger came in and the lettuce etc, she decided to make herself a little salad in the other half of her container. The five of us kids thought it was funny and this was made all the more funny when she went up and asked for salad dressing and a fork to eat her salad with. She must have been the inspiration for what would become the Salad Bar! The second restaurant story involves Banana Splits and five children with eyes that were bigger than their stomachs. We had stopped at a restaurant and while we ate, the five of us kids were looking at the desert menu and we asked our parents for Banana Splits for deserts. My parents answered with a no because for some reason we never got desert when we ordered out. However, Aunt Doreen being the best and greatest Spoiler decided that we could have the Banana Splits and she ordered one for each of us. The waitress however, wasn't the brightest bulb because she never mentioned that perhaps the Banana Splits weren't the best choice for children (especially if they had eaten within the last week) because these things were huge. I have never seen that much ice cream served to a single person in my entire life. When they were served we enthusiastically dove into eating the creations. However, they were just too big. Soon ice cream was melting and dripping down the sides of the bowls and onto the table. We had ice cream all over ourselves and the floor and the table. It was a huge disaster. Ironically, the name of the restaurant was the Shenandoah Restaurant. The Shenandoah was a blimp (like the Hindenburg) that had crashed in southern Ohio on September 2, 1925.

I can list some other examples and ways that Aunt Doreen would spend money on us and spoil us even more rotten than we already were. If we were in a store and said wow look at those Yo-Yos, we would get Yo-Yos. If we looked at bags of candy we would get a bag of candy and it wasn't just one bag to share among five of us instead it was a bag for each of us.

When she initially left the United States, Aunt Doreen stored several large trunks in our basement. Years later on one of her return trips, she opened those trunks and handed over to myself and my siblings the items that Uncle Bruce had treasured most in life. There weren't any great and rare items in that chest but what she gave us were mementos of an Uncle that we had lost way too soon. One of the things that she gave me was a small Bible that was in a case and fit into a pocket. It was a Serviceman's Bible. It was inscribed with Uncle Bruce's name and the dates that he served in the Army. She told me that she wanted me to have it because if I was ever to serve in the Military that Bible was to go with me. It was as if she knew that I would one day be serving in the military and even a war. I did carry it with me everyday that I ever wore my country's uniform. It was with me at Ft. Dix, NJ for basic training and Ft. Sam Houston, San Antonio, TX for Advanced Individual Training. It also went with me to Saudi Arabia for Desert Storm in 1990-1991. I later passed it onto my nephew Danny when he went to Iraq in 2005. He then passed it onto his son and it even has been passed onto his grandson. Traditions are great.

Another great memory about Aunt Doreen centers on Christmas. She wasn't much on writing letters or calling us when she was in England but she did write each year at Christmas with a card. Inside the card was always cash money to help pay for our Christmas celebration. Yes she sent cash through the mail. However, it was never the cash that we waited on (well never totally waited on the cash because it was always fun to receive it and spend it) – instead it was the amazing way that she always managed to get the card to arrive on the very last day of mail delivery before Christmas. So if Christmas Eve was a Monday through Saturday, that card always arrived on Christmas Eve – just like clockwork.

The gift that Uncle Bruce & Aunt Doreen gave to me was that I could succeed in this world and I could travel the world even though I was born in a small Ohio town. Uncle Bruce did it and so could I.

N'Edna

N'Edna was actually my dad's older sister Aunt Edna, however, kids being kids when we were little when we said her name it came out N'Edna and it stuck. N'Edna was one of those people who said exactly what she thought about a subject regardless of whether the person hearing her opinion was going to care or not care. That is what made her so great – you knew where you stood at all times for good or for bad but you knew where you stood. A perfect example of her being very blunt with her opinions was when I was moving into my second home. My brand new next door neighbor had come over to my house to introduce himself and when he rang the door bell, N'Edna answered the door because she was closest to the door. Unfortunately, as it turned out, my next door neighbor was an individual that N'Edna had had some business dealings with and she didn't like the man. So, instead of N'Edna calling me to the door, she simply told my neighbor to go away as she slammed the door in his face. It didn't matter to her that I had to live next door to the man. Nope! All that mattered was that she didn't like him and since she could she slammed the door in his face.

N'Edna was older than my dad by 12 years and since my parents were older when they started having me and my siblings and since Grandma Barton had died, N'Edna kind of became a surrogate grandmother to myself and my siblings. Fortunately, this was a really cool thing and I think we all benefited from the situation.

N'Edna used to cut my hair for me which also was a really cool thing because like any good barber, there was a lot of good conversation that occurred during those hair cuts (the sad thing is that I don't think that I have had a hair cut completely measure up since she passed away not because of the cut but because of the conversations). N'Edna filled me in on family history during those hair cuts. She would also give me advice – sometimes it was solicited advice and sometimes it wasn't but more times than not it was good advice. She told me stories about her antique cars and trips that she and her husband had gone on. She told me stories about traveling around the country during World War II with her husband, her daughter, my grandparents and my father. The stories that she told me about Grandpa Charlie and my dad were the type of stories that would eventually give me a lot of insight into why these men were the rough talking men of few emotions that they were. Through the use of her stories, she never excused their behavior but at least she sort of explained it.

She used to love to tell stories about me also. I think some of the details were made up because I just don't believe I could be as stubborn as she portrayed me to be. One of the stories was about when she would baby-sit my sisters, me and my brother for my parents. She said that the five of us would get to picking on each other and hassling with each other and then all out war would break out. Her solution was to sit us in a circle and make us look at each other until we resolved our issues. Well, this didn't sit well (no pun intended) with me so I would just get up from the circle and go about my business. N'Edna on the other hand had other ideas and she would march me back to my seat and sit me down. I would then get up and back and forth it would go until she literally had to sit down and hold me in that sitting position until I gave in. And to think she had the nerve to say I was stubborn, she was just as stubborn in that she wouldn't let me do what I wanted to do. All she had to do was let me do what I wanted but noooooooooo she was determined to hold me in place. I guess I came by my stubbornness honestly.

The other story about my stubbornness that she talked about was when my baby brother was born. She was staying at the house taking care of my sisters and myself while mom was in the hospital. I was too young to really realize that Mommy was there to have a baby or that a baby was coming home. At four years of age, I just knew my mom wasn't home and I wanted her home. So I would open the front door and stand there waiting for my mom. N'Edna would pull me away and shut the door and then before she could blink I would be back at the front door waiting on my mom. Every time that she told the story, she would always say that she thought I was going to drive her crazy. Also, there was another battle during this time. One night, I wanted my usual glass of milk before bed. The problem was N'Edna could not find my special milk cup to give it to me. The cup was a little white cup that Great Aunt Ruth had bought for me that had my name written on it. I always drank out of that cup at bedtime and for some reason she couldn't find it. She hunted and hunted but to no avail. She handed me another cup and I refused to drink the milk. I wanted my cup. She finally had had enough and she decided that if I was going to act like a baby she would treat me like a baby and she poured my milk into one of the new baby bottles that my mom had ready for when she brought the new baby home from the hospital. Well, when she handed me the bottle, I took one look at that and I told her that I wasn't a baby and that I wasn't going to drink out of a baby bottle. Her answer was drink or get to bed. So, being the bright child of 4 that I was, I emptied that bottle right away. No I did not drink it. I just poured it all over the floor. N'Edna stared in disbelief for about two seconds and then she spanked my bottom and put me in my bed. Guess what? I never ever pulled a stunt like that with her again.

I think the greatest thing that I got from N'Edna was determination (aka stubbornness). She used to tell me about Grandpa Charlie not allowing her to go to High School after she completed the 8th grade. She on the other hand was bound and determined to go to high school. She and Grandpa Charlie fought and argued until he finally decided to let her go provided that she would get all of her chores done before she would go to school. Of course, his plan was to give her too many chores so that she could never finish them or so that she would decide that it just wasn't worth doing that much work in order to go to school. She on the other hand was so determined that she would get up and do all of the assigned chores and then she would go off to school. He never let up for the four years she was in high school and likewise neither did she. Thank you N'Edna for the determination.

I know that I have written only about a few of my ancestors and I am sure that others gave me gifts too that I have used in life but these are some of the most important ones. I am grateful to all of them for each of the gifts that they gave to me and the lessons that they taught me that I have used throughout my lifetime. There are some more special relatives who also gave me some great gifts however, some of them are still alive and I opted to leave them out so that I can't embarrass them with any story I might share and also so as to prevent them from suing me if they feel that I don't portray them in an accurate light.

Chapter Two – Childhood Events

When I think about my childhood events, I have a lot of great memories. Memories that even after these many years still remain fresh in my mind. Most of these memories are centered in a little neighborhood in my hometown known as Fairhope.

I remember being a kid and thinking that Fairhope was the entire universe. It was great. Everyone knew everyone. There were no strangers there. We were able to go trick or treating on Halloween without fear of getting poisoned candy or a razor blade in an apple. You could talk to adults without fear of being kidnapped and molested.

We were able to play outside from morning to night, ride our bikes (without helmets) around the neighborhood and just be kids. I remember how much fun it was to ride my bike up Gephart (the street I lived on) to Daisy. The hill going up Gephart seemed huge and then we would ride to the top of Daisy which that hill seemed even larger and then turn around and ride down the hill (we even sometimes dared to ride down the hills without having our hands on the handle bars). It was amazing how those two hills seemed so huge and yet as I noticed later in life as an adult, neither of the hills were ever all that huge. As children, we would go down the street to Fairhope Elementary and swing, and slide down the sliding boards and climb on the monkey bars. Amazingly, after children had been playing on that playground equipment at Fairhope School since the 1920s, in 2008, the powers that be who ran the schools decided that Swings, Monkey Bars and Sliding boards were evil and they were removed from the playground. What a shame! The only time that playing on the playground wasn't safe was for a brief time when I was about 7 and there was a new bully in the neighborhood who decided that he at the age of 14 owned the playground and that if other kids wanted to play on it then we had to pay him for the privilege. However, the bully soon learned a very important lesson and that was that the kids in Fairhope didn't play that way. Every kid in the neighborhood got together and went to the playground to play. When the bully showed up to collect his playground fee, we all refused to pay up and we told him to leave. The bully then proceeded to push all of us kids around and we took off running. However it was a trick that we had planned for the purpose of lulling the bully into a false sense of superiority. The next day, we returned as a group. However, when we returned, we brought along two 17 year olds (older brothers of a couple of the kids in the neighborhood) who we had paid just to serve as our bodyguards.

I don't want to give the wrong impression because we didn't hire the 17 year olds to beat up the 14 year old bully. Instead we hired them to suggest to Mr. Bully that he should leave us alone. Unfortunately, Mr. Bully decided he was Mr. Badass and he wouldn't listen to reason. When he decided to shove a six year girl down, the 17 year olds grabbed him and they were ready to do some serious damage. Instead, one of the older girls suggested that we give the Bully a trial. So the 17 year olds tied the kid up to the monkey bars and a trial was held. The verdict – GUILTY! The punishment that he was given was to be decided by the six year old who he had knocked down. She decided he should be given a wedgie, followed by a dip in the ditch (the ditch was filled with some nasty scummy green water) and then finally flipped into the garbage dumpster.

The two 17 year olds grabbed him, untied him, and pulled so hard giving him his wedgie that the waist band on his underwear ripped clean off. Next, they grabbed him by the ankles and dipped him head first in the ditch of nasty water and finally they dumped him into the dumpster. By this time, Mr. Bully was screaming and crying and he took off running for home. The 17 year olds collected their fee and left just before Mr. Bully and his father returned to seek their revenge. Mr. Bully Sr. demanded to know who had beat up his son. Every kid on the playground yelled out in unison "she did" and we pointed at the six year old and she stood up and said "it was me!" Mr. Bully Sr. just looked at his son and dragged him home. Mr. Bully Jr. never bothered us again.

Another example of a memory involving the innocence of our community was the fact that we even had a Popsicle Man who would drive through the neighborhood during the summer and all we had to do was yell stop and for just a quarter we could get a cool treat. We used to call the Popsicle man the Jingle Jip guy if he came by and we didn't have any money. We would act like our friends who had money and could buy stuff were being ripped off because his prices were too high. In truth we were just jealous. I somehow doubt that in this day and age any parent would allow a child to buy a Popsicle off the back of a truck being driven by a stranger but who knows perhaps there are still some Popsicle Men out there hawking their icy treats on a hot a summer day to children they don't know.

Some other great examples of a simpler time and the innocence of the era:

We weren't afraid to drink out of a hose.

We didn't need a pool in the summer instead we loved to be squirted by the hose or just use a sprinkler to run through on a hot summer day in our swimsuits.

We built forts in the empty lot that my parents owned behind our house.

We climbed trees.

We ate green apples and wild berries.

We left our doors unlocked.

We played outside winter, spring, summer or fall.

We knew the names of every person living on our street.

Neighbors helped neighbors.

We had a bread man who would deliver fresh bread and baked goods to the house and he never knocked on the door but rather he just walked into the kitchen.

We had a dairy man who delivered milk, ice cream and other dairy products and he never knocked on the door either he also just walked into the kitchen.

I have so many great memories that I am hesitant to choose which memories were the greatest. Therefore, I have chosen to relate stories of my childhood that aren't sweet tender moments but rather what follows is a list of memories that probably bring the most laughs to me and are the least Presidential moments of my life.

The Vacation of Flushing the Toilet & Red Hot Dogs

When I was a young kid my parents only ever took my siblings and I on one vacation out of the State of Ohio. I don't know if the trip was such a disaster that they feared to ever do it again or if they never did again because they couldn't afford it but there was only one trip. The trip encompassed so many wonderful fond memories and then there were the parts of the story that mother would have gladly forgotten if it weren't for the fact that my father always told them over and over again because he thought they were funny.

One of the first stops was in Washington DC as we worked our way south along the eastern seaboard. Interestingly enough, this was the only time I was ever in DC until after I was elected President and I like to think I left my mark both times.

According to my father's story I as a young toddler of 3 during that first trip was fascinated by the toilet in our hotel room and I kept going into the bathroom to flush the toilet. My mother had left me in my father's care as she took my sisters shopping. According to my father he thought I was just flushing the toilet. While the constant flushing was annoying him as he attempted to watch a baseball game on the TV, he thought I wasn't hurting anything. In reality I was putting toys, soap, and anything else that I could get a hold of into the toilet and I was flushing the objects down the toilet or at least attempting to flush them down the toilet. By the time my mother returned to the room, the toilet was plugged and overflowing. I was soaked and the water was soaking into the actual hotel room. My mother was furious, the hotel staff wasn't very pleased, the guests downstairs were angry, my sisters were unhappy about their lost toys and my father was in deep trouble.

(Later when I went to Washington DC as the President, there were times when I would have liked to have flushed a lot of things and some Senators down the toilet when they started aggravating me.)

Still damp from the great DC flood caused by a three year old and inattentive father, the family headed for North Carolina to visit some relatives so distant that I can't even remember the names of the people. Typical of family reunions, as we arrived there was a whole lot of kissing and hugging with a whole lot of "it's been forever since we have seen each other but you haven't aged a bit." The North Carolina Bartons had arranged a picnic in our honor. Every relative from that neck of the woods had come to visit with the northern relatives and the buffet of covered dishes was spread out for all to partake. All that is except me and my sisters who wanted nothing to do with any of the food. We wanted hot dogs.

Our second cousin twice removed on our grandmother's sister's side who was serving as the hostess for the family reunion, just couldn't say no to four such cute little visitors from Ohio so she told everyone that they would just have to wait until she ran down to the supermarket to pick up some hot dogs for the cousins. She took off and returned just as quickly as possible and she cooked up those hot dogs for the four of us. However, there was one problem; the hot dogs weren't like our hot dogs in Ohio. These hot dogs were bright red and there was no way we were going to eat those things and we let it be known to all the North Carolina relatives. My mother was furious. How dare we not eat those hot dogs after this wonderful woman had gone to the extra trouble of getting them for us. This wasn't the first time or the last time that we misbehaved in a manor that disappointed our mother but it was the only time we did it outside of Ohio. I am proud to say though that our mother did manage to eventually teach us better manners and I never insulted another hostess by demanding special food or refusing to eat food that was prepared for me.

Sleepwalking

Up until I was about 10 years old, I would regularly sleep walk. I would wander about the house talking with my mom, my dad, and my siblings and yet be totally asleep. The following morning, I would have no memory whatsoever of having walked and talked in my sleep.

Luckily for me my mother was a light sleeper and whenever I would begin a nocturnal walk about the house after everyone had gone to sleep, my mother would get up and follow me around and she would eventually get me back to my own bed safe and sound.

However, one night that didn't quite happen and I scared my entire family. It was the middle of the winter and the temperature was well below freezing. I got up and my mother never heard me leave. This time, I managed to unlock the front door and I headed off to play at the playground at Fairhope Elementary school. I was wearing pajamas and no shoes but that didn't stop me. The next day everyone in the family and all of the neighbors were just amazed that walking on the cold snow didn't wake me up.

At about 2:15am, the man across the street who was a volunteer fireman and EMT came home from a squad call and as he pulled into his driveway he noticed that our front door was standing open. He knew something was up because nobody would have a front door open in the middle of a winter night like that one was. So he went over to our house and rang the door bell to wake my entire family. At first my father and mother thought that somebody must have broken into the house. However, my brother pointed out that I wasn't in the bedroom that we shared. Instantly my mother realized that I had wandered off and the search was on. Luckily for me they found me within a few minutes down at the playground swinging on a swing. They brought me back home and dried me off and put me back into bed and I never woke up until the next morning. At breakfast the next day, I was well rested and everyone else was extremely tired. When my mom told me what had happened, I was amazed and I just laughed because I couldn't believe that it had happened.

Of course that next morning my dad installed a new lock on the front door of the house that was well above my reach. Years later when my parents had passed away and we were attempting to sell their home, every potential buyer who looked at the house asked the same question "why is that lock so high on the door?" My standard answer was that it had been that way when we moved in and we never knew why.

I have often wondered why I had been a sleepwalker and then just suddenly quit without ever knowing why. Of course after I moved into my home and lived alone – who knows – I might have picked up the habit again and I wouldn't even know it since I never remembered a single incident of sleepwalking.

Roofers Hate Green Apples

One summer, a new house was being built on the empty lot next to the empty lot that my parents owned behind our house. I and my buddies loved to play on the construction sight but everyday the workers would chase us off because they were afraid we would get hurt. So, since we couldn't play on the construction site, we did the next best thing, and we would climb the apple trees on my parent's lot and watch the guys work. We especially loved it when they would cuss and swear – boys being boys we thought it was cool.

One day as my brother and I sat in our tree watching the roofers work on the hottest day of the summer, one of the kids that we didn't like from the neighborhood showed up and started bothering us. The poor kid was just a big old butterball and he was just downright annoying because he thought he was the fastest kid in the neighborhood. He even called himself the Zipster because of how fast he thought he could run. However, he couldn't climb a tree to save his own life. As my brother and I sat in the tree, Zipster kept trying to reach the bottom branch and drag his butterball butt up the tree and he kept slipping back down the tree trunk. Unfortunately for Zipster, one of the roofers took note of the kid's inability to climb the tree and the guy started making fun of the poor kid. Normally, we made fun of the kid ourselves but my brother and I decided that the roofer had no business making fun of the old Zipster so we climbed out of the tree and suggested that Zipster should throw some apples at the roofer in retaliation for the insults and jokes that the roofer was lobbing at Zipster. Of course, Old Zipster listened to our suggestion and he just started throwing the apples like a wild man.

Well old man roofer thought it was funny that some dumb kid was throwing apples at him and the fact that the kid couldn't hit the broad side of a barn just kept the roofer laughing like crazy. The funny part is that the roofer kept egging on old Zipster. This was all great fun so my brother and I decided we should throw some green apples too. Soon there were about 15 kids there and we were all throwing apples and the roofers were all laughing and having a great time until somebody got off a lucky throw and nailed the roofer who started this whole thing right between the legs.

Boy was he pissed! He was cussing and he told us all to stop right now or he would come down the ladder and kick our asses. Did we stop? Of course not and in fact somebody nailed the dude between the legs a second time. Down he came – ready to kill and we all took off running. My brother and I raced across the lot and across our backyard and dove through the back door of our garage and slammed it shut. Kids were running every which way just to get away. Poor old Zipster who thought he was so fast didn't quite live up to his own hype that day. He did make it to our back garage door that my brother and I were hiding behind after we had locked it. As we lay on the garage floor trying to catch our breaths and not shit our pants we just heard - Bang Bang Bang – which of course was Zipster. He was knocking on that door in desperation to save his life. "Let me in Let me in Let me in!" The utter fear in his voice was an eerie sound. Since he was banging and pleading for his life, I decided to look to see if it was safe to let him. Just as I looked out, I saw Roofer Dude grabbed old Zipster and pick him up so that he could look Zipster square in the eye in order to yell and cuss at that child for what seemed an eternity. Old Zipster was shaking and was as pale as pale could be.

As I stood there peering through the window, I caught the Roofer's eye and he must have decided that Old Zipster was too scared to comprehend the threats about not throwing any more apples so he decided to put his face right against the window and tell me that if one more kid threw even one more apple he would catch the kid and break the kid's arms. I just stared as he screamed "DO YOU UNDERSTAND?" I must have finally nodded my head as if to say yes because he finally put Zipster down and stormed back off to the roof.

I opened the door and Zipster sat there bawling and bawling. I also noted that his pants had a huge wet spot.

I learned a very important lesson that day let me tell you. If you are going to be in a dangerous situation and you think you will have to escape, you don't have to be the fastest runner, you just have to be faster than at least one other person.

The lesson that I didn't learn that day was that you should not poke a sleeping bear with a stick. Thirty minutes later we (the pack of kids minus Zipster) were back in the empty lot throwing green apples at the roofers. We would throw and hit them and they would cuss and start for the ladder and we would run away. Although, poking the sleeping bear with a stick proved to be somewhat fun that day and later in life as President I did it on more than one occasion, I should have learned that it was dangerous. We could have made one of the roofers fall off the roof and get hurt or we could have been seriously hurt by a roofer.

The Night I Ran Away From Home (Sort of)

It was a hot August night when I decided I couldn't take it on Gephart Avenue anymore and I decided to leave. However, at the time was I was only 6 years old and I wasn't the bravest kid in the world and I got scared so I never made it out of the front yard. Even though my running away didn't happen that night a whole series of events occurred that made the night quite memorable.

The evening started out with my mom taking my brother over to some friends so he could play with their young son who was his age. My mother then took my three sisters shopping for school clothes and that meant that I was left home with just my father. It was a typical scenario of me being left with my father – I was to stay out of his way while he worked on one of his projects and stay out of trouble and all would be good or else. His project that night was to mow the yard at our house and the empty lot that was behind our house. So he was mowing and I was just sitting there watching him. I was bored out of my mind. The neighbors came over and said they were going for a walk and wanted to know if I could go with them. My father's answer was "NO'. So they walked away and I continued sitting there watching my dad mow the yard. My resentment grew with each pass he made on the mower.

At one point he stopped went into the locked house and got himself a beer. He didn't even ask if I wanted something to drink. So when he walked back outside, I said "can I have some milk?" His answer was "NO you should have said something before I came back outside". He then proceeded to tell me to drink from the hose. I didn't want a drink from the hose, I wanted milk but pouting didn't work on my father and off he went to his mowing.

As I sat there brooding about his slight, I developed a plan. I would run away and then when my mom came home and I was gone he would be in trouble. The only problem was that I couldn't get into the house to get anything to take with me and I really was too scared to actually run away because of the stories my sisters had told me about Bigfoot (yet another form a torture they inflicted on me over the years – lets see the list included basements, Bigfoot, Tornadoes, the name thing, leaving me beside the road and the murder of Smokey the Bear & Bugs Bunny – more on these later maybe).

My solution to running away without leaving the safety of home was that I would just hide in the bushes in front of our house so HE couldn't find me and then when my mom came home I could watch her yell at him. The only part I hadn't figured out was how I would explain why I hadn't come out of the bushes if he started hunting for me before she came home. As I prepared to climb into the bushes, I simply thought - Oh well that was a minor detail. So into the bushes I climbed. Sure enough HE finished mowing and HE started to look for me. He was calling my name over and over and over. I just remained in that bush smiling because I was thinking that he was going to be in BIG trouble once my mother returned home. However, this is the part of the story where the events got out of my control (in fact a person might say that things spiraled out of control something akin to a tornado or a hurricane or any other disaster that you might imagine).

(Also, please note, this was actually somewhat a lesson in how to spin an Issue and I was able to put it to use as President of the United States of America later in life.)

Some of the neighbors heard my dad calling out my name and they came over to see if they could help. The neighbors quickly organized themselves. Men got in their cars; kids got on their bikes and every able body began scouring the neighborhood. Some of the women started going door to door knocking and asking if anyone had seen me and asking those people to search around their homes for me. Some of the other women even set up a "food station" thinking that the search was going to last all night or perhaps weeks. Coffee was made, a table set up, someone brought an ice chest with sodas, sandwiches were brought out on platters, and ovens were fired up with cookies and brownies being baked. Women started calling friends on neighboring streets. The man across the street in the tallest two story home in the entire Fairhope area climbed up his TV antenna tower and onto his roof with his binoculars so that he could scan the entire neighborhood.

These people were in full blown emergency mode. However, the worst was yet to come.

One of our neighbors who I will call Crazy Momma was a very eccentric, very skinny (120 pounds) & a very tall (6'5 inch) widow. I am sure that she only stayed that skinny because of nervous energy. I mean this woman could eat an entire ham in one sitting by herself and that ham would be picked clean to the bone! Crazy Momma had 12 kids and she lived in the largest house in the neighborhood. However, she never threw anything away and accordingly the house was bulging at every seam with stuff and the stuff overflowed from the house and out into the yard.

This woman was obsessed with her "stuff"; she knew where everything was and she could tell if anything (inside or outside) was even one inch out of place at just a glance. Just as obsessed as she was with her "stuff", she was equally obsessed with her children. She constantly had to know where they were and what they were doing. None of the 12 children were allowed out of the yard – they were home schooled by Crazy Momma (even before it was cool to home school your children which was around 2005). When Crazy Momma did venture out of their house and when she allowed the children to venture out with her they followed behind her youngest to oldest and they were all tethered to Crazy Momma by a rope. She was paranoid that all strangers wanted to kidnap one or all of her children. If anyone even looked at her children when they were out in public, she threatened to turn them into her best friend the county Sheriff. The neighborhood was never sure of whether or not she was more worried about her "stuff" or her children. So when she heard that a child was missing out of the neighborhood it sent her into a tizzy fizzy fit. She locked all of her children into their rooms and she became a woman on a mission.

She arrived at the command center/food station and between sandwiches that she shoved down her throat, she proclaimed for the entire neighborhood to hear that she was sure that I been kidnapped. She was crying and sobbing and just going on about how devastated she would be if she lost one of her own 12 kids. She kept saying "what are the Bartons going to do without what's his name." She was so hysterical that she said she couldn't remember my name. Yet she sure could eat. (Oh yeah did I mention that from my vantage point in the bush that I was hiding in I could see and hear all of this!) Even at 6 years of age, I knew it was time for this to stop! I was just getting ready to climb out of the bush and take my punishment when a Stark County Sheriff's car pulled up and stopped.

Crazy Momma had called her friend the Sheriff before she had come over to graze on the buffet. Guess who stepped out of the Sheriff's car? Was it a deputy? Oh no the Sheriff himself and then three more sheriff's cars pulled up and so at that point there standing in the street in front of our house was the Sheriff and 6 deputies all on the case of the supposed kidnapped kid.

Now at this point of the story I wished that I had actually run away because it was now a full blown disaster that was going to get even worse.

It was a very bad thing that the Sheriff and his deputies had shown up. Yet it wasn't quite bad enough and the next step down disaster lane was the fact that the volunteer fire department showed up. Lights, Sirens, Action – men in fire coats and fire boots were running here and there all in the name of finding and saving the missing boy (who was really in the bush 50 feet away and was watching the show)!

In the midst of all that excitement, finally my mother and sisters pulled into the driveway. The lady who was supposed to be angry with my father when this all started was now scared to death because of the police cars and the fire trucks. Naturally to further complicate things the first person that reached my mom was none other than Crazy Momma (who had started the kidnap rumors). She grabbed my mom and practically yanked her out of the car and she started telling my mother that I had been kidnapped and that "somebody" had now reported that it had been three men in a junky car that had grabbed me and that in spite of all that, my mom should just relax because the sheriff was there. Of course this only caused my mother more panic and it ruined any hope of my dear sweet caring mom ever fixing this problem.

I didn't know what to do but pray. Suddenly, one of my mom's best friends sat down on the stoop to our house that was right next to my bush aka my secret hiding place aka soon to be tomb. My heart was beating so fast, I was sure that she would see me or hear me and then turn me in but she didn't and soon she stood up and left. My mind was racing until I decided I needed to go to sleep and I needed to go to sleep instantly. I figured if I could convince everyone that I had climbed into the bush and I had fallen asleep, then I couldn't get in trouble for hiding. So I lay down and feigned being sound asleep. The only trouble was nobody returned to sit on the stoop. How was I supposed to let them know I am in the bush so that I could be found if I am supposed to be asleep? Finally the lady who had sat on the stoop returned to her seat but she wouldn't look down and notice me so I rolled over like a kid would do in his sleep. Still she didn't notice me. I had to roll over like 100 times before she finally looked down. She grabbed me and yelled that she had found the lost child. Everyone came rushing to me, my mom hugged me and cried and everyone was rejoicing. Then the Sheriff came over and he started to question me. "Why didn't you answer when everyone called your name?" I just acted like an innocent little angel and kept repeating "what are you talking about? I was sleeping and I took a nap!" I wasn't sure that anyone was buying that act as I played my role of an innocent child and I knew the Sheriff didn't buy it and even worse was the fact that I knew my father definitely didn't buy it.

After a very stern lecture the sheriff and his deputies departed and slowly the neighbors started returning to their homes (even as I silently pleaded with God for the neighbors to stay and finish the food at the buffet so that there would be witnesses; which I hoped might prevent my father from punishing me). Unfortunately the "witnesses" left and that is when I got yelled at by my father like no kid has ever gotten yelled at before or since. Luckily, my mom eventually intervened just as the big brown belt was about to be removed and she defended me by saying that I had fallen asleep and that the adults had overreacted and that he needed to forget about it. Thank god for moms and thank god she bought that "I fell asleep routine!"

Babysitters

Another great memory of childhood were babysitters. Most of the teenagers in our neighborhood who hired themselves out to be babysitters believed that once the parents left then they could act and behave as if they were absolute dictators. They loved to tell you "no snacks" or "we were going to watch what the babysitting Goddess wanted to watch on TV" etc. Unfortunately, for the babysitters, my siblings and I never met a babysitter we couldn't easily get rid of. We would always employ our full arsenal of weapons to terrorize the babysitters. Some of our tactics were more drastic than others and perhaps we went to far from time to time. As a result of some of our tactics, I often wondered over the years how many of them had to seek out therapy after a night in our home.

Let's see if I can remember some of the babysitters. Our first babysitters were the girls next door Carlene & Sherlyne. Neither one of them wanted to be alone with us and neither one wanted to spend an entire evening at our mercy so they would do split shifts. Carlene and a friend (bodyguard) would come over for the first half as my parents left. Then after a few hours of chasing us around and screaming at us. Sherlyne and a friend would come in and relieve Carlene and her friend. We never really victimized these young ladies because they lived right next door and their parents could very easily be called over to stop the madness when we went too far.

However, after the sisters, we had one babysitter after another who all became one night wonders! One even deserted us mid shift and our parents returned home to find us alone. One of the one night wonders accidentally was locked in a closet and she spent the whole night there. However, when our parents came home they found the house neat and tidy and all of us sound asleep in our beds as if we had been properly supervised the entire evening. The closet door had been opened just prior to our parents coming home and yet the sitter was still inside. According to my mom, the sitter was curled up in the fetal position sucking her thumb. Our parents asked why she was in the closet like that and she said we had locked her in. My father took her home and the next day we were asked if we had locked her in and a choir of 5 angelic voices sang out "No – she was acting strange after she drank one of dad's beers and that she went into the closet and wouldn't come out so we went to bed." She never babysat in the neighborhood again because Mom bought that story in part because we had opened a beer and poured it down the drain so that there would be an empty bottle waiting on the kitchen counter for our parents to discover and since it was my father's beer, we knew that he would know that one had been emptied and that it hadn't been emptied by him.

Then there was Terrible. Terrible was the worst babysitter experience for myself and my brother. My sisters actually liked her, while my brother and I strongly disliked her. So our sisters turned on us and it was two against four. However, my brother and I won out after I used my Polaroid camera to get evidence of Terrible and her boyfriend doing things in my parents' bed while she was supposed to be watching us. After that, Terrible towed the line.

The best thing about having babysitters that were afraid of us was the fact that we could invite friends over and eat whatever we wanted to and make prank phone calls. This of course was before caller ID & Star 69, so nobody could trace our calls. In addition, they were prank calls not obscene calls. We would do the usual calls such as "is your refrigerator running?" "yes" "well you better go catch it." Although one time we did do something unique with our phone pranks. It was a weekday and we had a sitter so we called a Pest Service. My sister asked the gentleman "do you get rid of all pests?" The man said "yes". So my sister says "can you get rid of my little brother?" The man suggested she call the cops and hung up on her. A final example of a typical call involved us calling a house and asking is "Fred" home. The person on the other end of the phone would say "no" and then we repeated this over and over until finally one of us would call and say "Hi this is Fred do I have any messages?" Yes I know it was lame but back in the day it was fun and exciting.

 Now I know a lot of this babysitter talk sounds like we were criminals or horrible people but in reality it is pretty mild compared to the horrors and the crimes that even children commit anymore.

Church & Making Jesus Happy!

Most of the babysitting episodes were followed the next morning by going to church to repent for our behavior. Actually, most of the time it wasn't really to repent but rather just coincidence that my parents only went out on Saturday nights so going to church just followed naturally.

Church when we were growing up was at the same Presbyterian church that my mother and her parents had always attended in Canton, Ohio. It was the church where my parents had been married and each of us kids had been baptized. It also was the church that my father was only in a total of 5 times in his life (once for his wedding to mom, four times for the baptisms of his children (Trudy & Lindy were twins) and for Trudy's wedding). So basically, our religious education fell on our mother's shoulders.

There were many times that I think my Mom was not too happy with being the solo parent in church. This was because as usual the Barton 5 could be quite the handful even in church. If we weren't talking or asking her a million questions, we were pinching and poking at each other as we squirmed about in our seats. I can still remember seeing several of the more dignified and refined parishioners (you can read that as Old Bats, I mean Blue Haired Women and their dutiful baldheaded husbands) give our family the once over and there were several dirty looks directed towards my mother as if to say "children (or perhaps just my mother's children) don't belong in church." After all, the Presbyterian Church is a pretty main line straight laced denomination. Presbyterians pretty much go to church, sit in their pews, sing the selected hymns, listen to the sermon, do their responsive readings, pray as indicated in the weekly program, and call it a day.

As an active eight year old boy, I thought it was stuffy and boring. I would complain each and every Sunday, begging my mother to let me stay home but she would never give in. However, in the summer of 1973, I changed my mind and I was grateful for the calm serenity of the Presbyterian Church and I stopped complaining about it.

On a random August Sunday morning in 1973, our Mother decided out of the blue to take us to another church on a Sunday morning. The new church of choice was the Church of the Divinity of the

New Christianity that was led by the Good Reverend Jethro T. (he never said his last name and I don't think anyone ever knew it – he just went by the Good Reverend Jethro T). The church was in an old run down church building that hadn't seen a congregation since the late 1940s and it was located at the end of our street in Fairhope.

As much as the building was run down and looking sad, the Good Reverend Jethro T. was always dressed to the nines in the most expensive suits that contributions & love offerings could buy and he was always wearing multiple diamond rings on several of his fingers. He had an "insurance salesman's smile" and everything about him was bigger then life, including his six foot four 450 pound frame. He even managed to complete the look by topping it off with a really bad toupee.

People all over the county were coming to his church to witness the show that he always gave to the congregation. Half the people were coming only to watch the show. The other half of the people that showed up came because they truly believed in the Good Reverend Jethro T. They believed that he could touch them and heal them of their sins, their health problems, their money problems and all other ailments.

His services were filled with action and drama. Audience participation was encouraged and the "true believers" never failed to participate. His favorite phrase of all was to say "today we are going to make Jesus Happy!" He would yell and scream his message as if he thought that he could shout the devil out of the sinners. As always, he ended the services by asking those who were feeling the call of Jesus to come down front to be baptized in order "to make Jesus happy!" Whenever he called for those in need of baptism and the laying on of hands for healing, it also signaled to the really true believers that it was time to get up and dance around in joy. They would twirl and spin and raise up their hands to the Glory of God. The louder that the Good Reverend Jethro T. would preach and the more he called out for volunteers to come forward to dedicate their lives to Christ, the more excited the true believers became. On that particular Sunday, one very old decrepit believer slowly drug herself down to the front, walking hunched over with her cane and then as she got to the front she dropped the can and fell to the floor rolling around. The Good Reverend Jethro T. seemed quite pleased with her performance and he kept saying "look at Mrs. C, the Holy Spirit has truly come upon her!" Each time he mentioned her name she rolled around even more – eventually she worked herself into such a frenzy that her dress was up over her head, exposing her slip. It was a sight to be seen (not). Then two other old ladies decided they had to get into the act and they were down in front jibber jabbering in what sounded like some nonsense language. The Good Reverend's response was that "the Holy Spirit has truly come upon Mrs. Z & Mrs. F too for they are talking in tongues!" He went on to say "Jesus is Happy today!"

Now that he had everyone stirred up to a frenzy, he called for his deacons to step into the baptismal pool (an old children's swimming pool that was about 5 feet in diameter and 4 feet deep. He had the deacons in the pool to perform the actual baptisms because he wasn't about to get his snazzy suit all wet. As the new converts stepped forward, the congregation stood to watch the dipping of the sinners to be born again into the glory of God or at least into the glory of God as according to the Good Reverend Jethro T. I couldn't see what was going on so I wandered on down to the front of the church. Unfortunately, the Good Reverend Jethro T. saw me and decided that I had come down to be baptized. He grabbed my arm and was pulling me up onto his platform to hand me off to his deacons for the dipping.

I was scared because I didn't want to be dipped and I was struggling to get away from this giant man, when I heard my mother yelling that he shouldn't baptize me. She kept saying "put my son down, he has already been baptized" but he kept pulling on my arm and I kept trying to pull away from him. Suddenly, he lost his grip on me and SPLASH he fell backwards into the Baptismal pool. The tidal wave that his 450 pounds set off soaked the first 10 rows of the congregation (sort of like Shamu at SeaWorld). Women and children were screaming. The non-believers were howling with laughter and I was in a state of shock. The only thing I could think of doing was to start running and run I did. I ran up the center aisle of the church and out of the doors. I was running for home and kept saying to myself, "thank God I am a Presbyterian and I will never complain about having to go to "our" church again." That day, I learned I was never to be a Holy Roller! For the next several years, after that whenever I saw the Good Reverend Jethro T. around the neighborhood, I always got the feeling that he had never gotten over the pool incident and I was sure that he wasn't looking at me in a Christian Way. Eventually, the Good Reverend Jethro T. ended up in prison for fleecing his flock and the building that housed the Church of the Divinity of the New Christianity burnt to the ground when it was struck by lightning.

Neighborhood Children – Friends & Enemies

Growing up in our neighborhood meant one day you could be friends with a kid and the next day you would be mortal enemies with the same kid. In fact, this could change from hour to hour. However, there were no kids' friends or siblings that were closer than myself and my siblings. I could say anything I wanted about my sisters or my brother but nobody else could or they were in trouble if they did.

However, out of the 5 of us, my oldest sister was the best defender of the Barton Five. I don't think Cathy ever took any crap from anyone her whole life. Once when she was about 8 years old she was out front jumping rope and minding her own business when one of Crazy Momma's daughters showed up at our house to play. It was the one and only time that Crazy Momma (see story of running away) allowed one of her children to come over to our house to play. Well CM's daughter decided she wanted to jump rope with Cathy. However, Cathy had a problem with sharing (she simply didn't want to share so she wouldn't do it). So, CM's daughter grabbed the jump rope out of Cathy's hands and as she grabbed the rope, Cathy fell down and skinned her knee on the sidewalk. This of course angered Cathy so she grabbed the jump rope back and she took her retribution. She grabbed CM's daughter, threw her down on the ground and straddled the girl. She then grabbed the jump rope and hog tied her like a cowboy tying up a steer in a rodeo. Then she just stood there yelling at CM's daughter saying "let's see you jump rope now!"

Another time that Cathy took matters into her own hands to defend herself and her siblings was after the Christmas of 1975. There was this kid who lived up the street by the name of Dudley. Dudley was the product of his mother's brief fling with a man other than her husband. For whatever reason, his mother had always been very honest with him that his father had been someone other than her husband. I was never sure how a person could have that conversation with a small child yet she had had that very conversation with her son. As a result even though he was a half sibling to his parents' other six children he always thought of himself as an only child. Accordingly, he thought he was something special and he spent a lot of time bossing around his mother's other children as he referred to them. As a result over the years, he thought he could do what he wanted to do and do it whenever he wanted to do it.

As always his mother out of guilt of the affair that produced him spoiled him and for Xmas 1975 she bought him a ten speed bike. So the brilliant child that he was he decided to ride it on Xmas day.

The only problem was there was three feet of snow outside. This of course amused my siblings and me to no end to watch the genius trying to peddle through the snow. So what did we decide to do? We decided that we would pelt the dude with snowballs as he tried to ride that bike down the road. He of course didn't like that idea. So he got off his bike and began to chase us. Being the intelligent young man that he was he left the bike in the middle of the street. As he was chasing us and not catching us, we continued to throw snowballs at him which of course enraged him further. This was all in great fun until the snowplow barreled down the street, plowing over his new bike destroying it beyond recognition. The snow plow driver never even stopped. Well, Dudley just snapped at that point. He started yelling and cussing at us and tried even harder to catch us. Unfortunately, for my younger brother, Dudley managed to get a hold of him.

Fortunately, for my brother, Cathy jumped in. She who was 13 grabbed Dudley who was 17 and a boy and pushed him up against the garage of our house and she used him like a punching bag. Bam Bam Bam her fists slammed against his face and with each punch his head banged against the garage door. This went on for what seemed like forever until my father came outside to see what was going on because he could hear Dudley's head banging against the garage door inside of the house.

My sister finally let go of Dudley and my father ordered him home. Poor Dudley never bothered any of us again. Cathy was our defender and the legend was born – mess with one Barton and you did it at great personal risk.

Another example of us as children being mean and tough on other kids in the neighborhood was the terrorizing of a set of triplets (two boys and one girl) who had moved into our community from Arkansas. We thought they were very annoying because they would just show up without warning and without an invitation.

The triplet Arkansas nuts would ask all sorts of questions and constantly tell us how much better Arkansas was in comparison to Ohio.

One day there were some birds flying around late in the evening and the female Arkansas Nut screamed thinking the birds were bats. She was frightened and as a result she scared her brothers. They took off running for home and an idea was born. We decided (actually, I think my sisters said) that the next time they came over we would tell them the bats were our pets and that we could call them whenever we wished by whistling for the bats. Now as lame as that sounds, it worked. The next evening after dinner we were in the backyard playing and here came the Arkansas Nuts and we told them to go home. They of course didn't want to so one of my sisters started whistling; this eerie creepy whistle. One of the boy Arkansas Nuts asked "what is she doing" and my other sister kind of shrugged and said "calling our pet bats." Well the three Arkansas Nuts took off running and the remainder of that summer it worked every time. Arkansas Nuts arrived, they annoyed us, and my sister whistled her creepy whistle and Arkansas Nuts would run home screaming.

The following summer their parents bought them a huge Saint Bernard dog that scared us to no end and the bats were forgotten. Lesson learned – in an arms race bigger is better.

Our next foray into neighbor to neighbor relations was when a few of the young girls in the neighborhood started smoking when they reached Junior high. My siblings and I thought this was horrible and we decided we would punish them by not playing with them. However, that entire summer when we would get bored, we would call the Smoking Club up and "apologize" and invite them over to play. However, before we would invite them over we would drag the garden hose into the house and then when we called we would just say that we were playing in the basement and that they should just come on in the front door. Of course when the members of the Smoking Club opened up the front door we would hose them down. As they ran home, we would just scream that we wanted to make sure their cigarettes were out and not burning because our parents didn't allow kids to smoke in the house. (As a side note: my parents were either progressive or without a clue on the kids smoking thing. They always told us that whenever we wanted to smoke like our father, we could. We just needed to let them know and we could do it as long as we smoked at home and that they knew. If it was a strategy, it worked. Not a one of us ever smoked.) Anyway all of those girls must have been the most gullible people on the planet because they accepted about 100 fake apologies and each time they were squirted with the hose. They were gullible and we were mean.

Summertime

Swim lessons, camping, rooftop tennis & picnics and one indoor water fight.

During my pre-teenage years, summers days were spent either going to work with my father or spending days at the campground where my parents kept our camper. Spending the summer at the same campground was cheaper than taking a real vacation and we got to do all the fun stuff – such as fishing & swimming, riding bikes & putt putt golf. The amazing thing was that my parents would leave the Barton Five at the campground all day by ourselves without a designated babysitter. However, there were enough old ladies and old men who also spent their summers there that we had plenty of eyes watching over us and that kept us somewhat in check.

We ran from sunrise to sunset those summer days at the campground. We were even allowed to go swimming without an adult accompanying us into the pool area which was Rule Number

One for all kids at the campground. Why were we given special dispensation? Well when we first starting camping, my mom made us take swimming lessons that were offered at the campground every summer by the American Red Cross. The lessons were the first week of June and at first we hated them because of the cool June mornings and the cold water. However, even though we complained a lot, we ended up enjoying the lessons and all five of us took to the water like naturals. I am proud to say we went from Beginner swimmers to the Advanced swimmers the first summer. So, because of our swimming abilities we were allowed in the pool whenever it was open. We were such regulars that we even got to be the "victims" when the lifeguards practiced rescues. Also, every couple of hours the lifeguards would clear the pool and do a safety check looking for anyone that might have drowned (I actually think it was just their way of getting to swim instead of sitting on their chairs) and we were allowed to swim with them in search of dead bodies.

The most amazing fact of those days is that we actually managed never to cause any permanent damage to ourselves or others. Plus nobody ever died. Not even myself when I tried a dive off the high diving board just because I wanted to be like the older boys in the pool. The teenagers that summer were doing this crazy dive where you flipped over the end of the high diving board and would hang from the end of it. Then you would pull yourself back up so that your feet were against the underside of the board and you kicked off diving into the water. Well, I came within inches of drilling myself into the cement platform that the diving board was attached to because when I pushed off I pushed towards the platform instead of away from the platform. Had I drilled myself into that cement, I would have either died or been a paraplegic. I managed to give the lifeguards that were on duty the biggest scare of their lives. One of the lifeguards (a guy named Michael who as a kid I thought was the coolest and I guess you could say was a role model to me) took me aside and had a serious man to man chat after my near fatal dive. First of all I learned at that point that peer pressure was dangerous and he told me that I should never again try to do something just because I wanted to be as cool as I thought someone else was. Second, he broke the news to me that I wasn't going to be an Olympic diver! Good advice and truthful advice! To some extent, I think that is why I was able to serve as President for eight years without ever worrying that some of the supposedly most important people in the country disagreed with my policies. I did what I thought was best and right for the majority not the select few. For the next couple of years, Michael was like a big brother to me and I never tried another stupid dive again.

When we weren't in the pool we were racing around the park on our bikes. Chasing each other or hiding from each other. We also loved to go to the Pastime Inn (where they had pinball machines, pool tables and a jukebox). The teenagers thought that we shouldn't be there but we were tolerated because the teenage boys that worked in the park mowing and cleaning vouched for us and put out the word that we were allowed to be there and nobody was to touch us. What was really fun was when a "new" kid would come into the place and see us little kids there and they would attempt to pick on us. Well if one of the workers from the park was there then usually the new kid ended up taking off running in fear of his life or the bully ended up terribly embarrassed in some other form. A couple of the older kids also would use us to win money off the new kids. All five of us could play pool and play it well. So, we often were put head to head with the new kids and we would always beat them.

The only time we almost got in trouble in the Pastime Inn was when we jammed the juke box with pennies so that it just kept playing the same song over and over. The song was the The Streak and if you have never heard it you aren't missing anything magical because it was just one of those songs that seemed funny the first time you heard it and it became a fad but in reality it wasn't all that great. In addition, it wasn't great when you heard it over and over and over. When the owner of the campground finally figured out what was wrong with the Jukebox he was on the hunt. Thank god he never found out it was us because he was also the Chief of Police in the little town where the campground was and we were afraid he would have arrested us. In fact even as I write this so many years later, I hope that the statue of limitations has run out on that crime.

In fact because the man liked us, we once got to go on a ride along when he and his deputies did a drug raid on a pot farm that was just down the road from the campground (yes I know it was crazy that he took five young children along but he did and to us it was exciting). That was the first time and last time I ever saw a pot plant in my entire life.

Another summer I also got to see for the first and last time ever in my life a cult at the campground and some gypsies in our hometown.

I don't really know if it was a true blue cult but all of the adults said it was and the group sure acted strangely. There were about 100 young adults (late teens into their 20s). They all slept in tents and they all dressed pretty much the same. They stayed in their own section of the campground and they wouldn't speak to anyone. They would get up in the morning and do group exercises and then in one giant group they would run down the hill to the bathroom and do their thing. Then they would run back as a group to their tents and change into their clothes which seemed to be more of a uniform since it was the same exact outfit. Next, they would get on the several old school buses that they traveled in and off they would go for the day. I don't remember if anyone knew where they went and what the did during the day but they left at the same time and returned at the same time each and every day.

When they returned in the evening, they would do group exercises again and then they would eat dinner and then the thunderous herd would run together to the bathroom. It was just so strange.

The gypsy story is another interesting story. They invaded the little town of Louisville one Saturday morning. There were about 50 of them and they were just swarming all over town. They were also stealing everything that wasn't nailed down. I was at the IGA with my mother and we witnessed a woman shove a watermelon up under her dress. As she started to leave the store, the manager of the store accused her of stealing and he gave chase. When they reached the parking lot, she stopped and turned towards the store manager and suddenly just lifted up her dress and the watermelon fell out and shattered on the parking lot. The whole time she kept saying she was cursing the manager for chasing her. The police finally arrived and escorted them out of town. Up until this point of time, I had heard stories about gypsies (such as the one that my mother always told about the Queen of Gypsies dying in Canton once upon a time) but this was the first time I had ever seen one and when I finally saw one I really saw one since she had lifted her dress up over head and she must have forgotten her undergarments that day because the only thing under her dress was skin and that watermelon!

For fun in the evenings at the campground we (the Barton Five) had two little activities that we would engage in. One was that we would wait for some one to go into the port a john to do their business and then we would sneak up on the port a john and place a stick in the clasp that was used to lock the port a john's when they weren't in use. It was great fun when the unsuspecting victim would try to leave the stinky smelly nasty port a john and they couldn't. They would beat on the door and scream until someone finally rescued them. The only rule – we could do it to anyone else but never to one of our own. The second game was to go to the area of the campground where the "over nighters" were always parked. We would wait for them to go inside and as they sat in the campers with the lights on we would run up and turn off their water and unplug their electricity. Then we would hide to wait for them to come out and reconnect. We usually did it twice to everyone because the first time they were angry but the second time they would be cussing and threatening the lives of whoever was doing it. We only did it to the over nighters because we knew in the morning they would be gone and we wouldn't see them again.

One other interesting thing about our camping adventures was the fact that one of my mom's best friends in the campground claimed that she could tell people their futures. Luckily for me she was off base on mine. She said that I would have an accident to my hands and that I would die in a foreign country. Well to this day (my 100th birthday), I haven't had a major accident to my hands and I have been to a lot of foreign countries and I am still alive. I guess I will just keep hanging out here in the good ole US of A at this point in my life and maybe I won't die.

As we grew older and stopped camping, we had to entertain ourselves in the neighborhood. We weren't allowed beyond a certain part of the neighborhood on our bikes but that never stopped us. We often got on our bikes and rode into Louisville to either the Dairy Queen or later McDonalds. Had our parents known how far we traveled on our bikes, they would have chained us to our beds but they didn't know and we were never chained to our beds.

Speaking of our parents being angry with us if they had known all we had done, I think we might have been shipped off to Military School or perhaps reform school if they had known about our secret adventures.

One such secret adventure was that we used to go to the elementary school that was at the end of our street and have picnics and play tennis. However, what was adventurous about it was it was all done on the roof of the school building. We would take the bike rack put it up on end and use it like a ladder to get on the lower roof. Then we would climb the ladder that was permanently attached to the higher part of the building from the lower part of the building and when we were up on that roof, we had our own little world.   Surprisingly, we were never caught doing this. Only one time did we ever come close to getting caught and that was when my sister cut her arm climbing onto the roof. We didn't think it was bad but as we returned home one of the neighbors freaked out and called the ambulance to take her to the hospital. Our mother was called at work and then we knew we were going to be busted as soon as she arrived at the hospital because my sister was going to have to say that she cut it climbing onto the roof. Somehow, my sister came up with a lame story about tripping on the old rusty sliding board at the playground and my parents bought it. Of course it cost my sister a tetanus shot but it was worth it to keep a Barton Five secret.

One final secret that our parents never knew about was the indoor water fight. It only occurred one time and that one time was bad enough. On a very hot August day, things got out of hand with an outside water fight and it eventually spilled over into the house. By the time it was finished everything was soaked in the entry hall of the house. The floor, the walls and the ceiling. Luckily it never went any further and none of the furniture got wet. We did have to scramble to dry the walls and the floors before the parents got home. We even had blow dryers out. It was yet another near miss and no butts beaten until they bled buttermilk.

Going to Work With My Dad

Back in the 70's there wasn't a whole lot of control over what
parents could or couldn't do with their children and accordingly,
sometimes my father would wake me up in the early morning
hours of the summer and drag me off to work with him. As early
as the age of 7, I would spend some of my summer days on
construction sites.

Oh the things I learned by going to work with my dad who was a
self employed carpenter and who sub contracted off a high end
home builder. Sadly, I never learned about carpentry. What did I
learn? Let's see:

1. I learned how to swear! The men on those construction
   sites could use the F word as nouns, verbs, adjectives and
   adverbs.

2. I learned all the proper and the not-so-proper terminology for
   a woman's anatomy and what men like to do with those
   pieces parts and I learned this in graphic terms.

3. I learned lots of dirty jokes – the only problem was I really
   didn't understand them but I could remember them and
   certainly could repeat them (sometimes at the most
   inappropriate moments).

4. I learned about bars! Every night on my father's trip home
   from work, he would stop at a bar called the Round House.
   It was the Round House because it was close to what was
   known as the round house for the Railroad (I don't know
   what that was – if you want to know – look it up because I
   don't care). Anyway, even when I was with him he still
   stopped in for a beer (or more). In we would walk and the

old barmaid who was usually drunk as a skunk would plop a beer in front of my dad and then give me a cola. All of my dad's cronies would be sitting on their assigned stools and then the stories would start. Not a one of my father's old cronies even pretended to act like I (a child) was in the room. The dirty words just flowed out of their mouths. Usually one of my father's associates (drunken friends) would buy me a candy bar or a bag of chips or give me money to play the Pinball machine. So there I was sitting on a bar stool in a cheap bar that always had that stale beer and cigarette smoke smell to it (it is a wonder that I didn't get Black Lung from the smoke) at the young age of 7. The education I got. The funny thing was when we went out to get in the truck to go home, my father would always say "don't tell Mommy that we stopped there – Ok?" and he would smile like we were best buddies sharing a secret. I never did say anything and was never sure if my mom knew or not. However, about the time I turned 10, I knew my mom knew because one night when my family had been out Christmas shopping my dad decided to stop by the Round House on the way home. He took my mom, my sisters, my brother and me into the bar. The bar was having its Annual Christmas Party for all the regulars. As we walked in all of the "Associates" yelled out my name just like they did after work. I was being greeted not as a son of their friend Don but as one of them. They all wanted to buy me a drink and candy bars like every other night. They were happy to see me. My mom on the other hand was not happy to witness my "homecoming" and dad wasn't happy that he was busted.

My First Business and My First Death Threat!

My parents would always put in a huge garden every summer. I think it was the only way to balance the food budget for a family of

7. For the most part what wasn't eaten fresh was put away into the freezer or canned to be used all winter. However, one year we had planted so much corn that it was going to go to waste. So my Dad decided that I should set up a stand in front of the house and sell the corn. So I got up really early and I picked the fresh corn and set up a card table at the edge of the street at the end of the driveway. I placed signs at both ends of the street and I spent the entire hot August day selling corn to every whacko that came up or down the street. I was selling the corn for a dollar for 13 ears of corn yet some of the more thrifty whackos would stop and ask for 15 ears at a dollar or they wanted 13 ears for seventy-five cents. The day was long, hot and boring but at least I had sold a lot of corn and had made some money.

However, right as I was getting ready to close up shop for the evening this 20 something dude came barreling up the road in his Chevy Nova (it was a hot car back in the 70s). He pulled up and asked me how much I was charging for the corn. So, I told him and he told me to hand him an ear so he could examine it. I handed him the ear and he told me "thanks for the corn kid" and he drove off while he laughed at me. I was mad – how dare he steal my corn after I had picked it and had sat there selling it all day. As I sat there stewing, I heard his loud Nova coming back down the street. So, the usually timid boy that I was decided to suddenly become a 10 year old man of action, so I stepped out into the middle of the road and put up one hand in front of me and the other behind my back and I screamed "STOP IN THE NAME OF THE LAW CORN THIEF!"

Well, I got the thief's attention and he slammed on the brakes and he came to a screeching halt just inches from hitting me. The dude was angry and he jumped out of his car and came running up to me. I calmly asked for the money for the corn or for the ear of corn back that he had stolen. This of course pissed him off more. So he decided to give me back the ear of corn however, he made mention that he was going to return it somewhere on my body that I didn't think was going to be comfortable. So as he returned to me with that ear, I decide to strike first. I kicked him in the balls and dropped him to the ground. I was smart enough to take off running for the house before he could regain his breath and he was smart enough to get back into his car when my father came out the front door. He drove off but he was angry. The remainder of the summer whenever he would see me outside playing when he drove up or down the street he would stop his car and chase me. It was scary but I learned a couple of lessons.

David sometimes slays Goliath (me kicking him in the balls) and sometimes David has to retreat to fight another day. After all these years, I wonder if Nova Dude ever had any kids!

Second Business
Casino Basement!

Since my parents both worked and most of the other mothers were stay at home moms, as we got older, a lot of the neighborhood kids looked forward to hanging out at our house without parental supervision during summer vacation and after school during the school year. While at our house, they weren't forced to clean their bedrooms, talk nice, and they could do the goofy things kids loved to do and even say a few swear words without fear of correction. The TV was always on and never tuned to the soap operas like their mothers always watched.

Downstairs in our basement, we had a pool table and my dad had a great poker table. So, logically, we allowed the other kids to play poker and pool but at a cost. Pool games were a dime and they the players had to place wagers as to who would win. The house (the Barton Five) took a cut of all wagers. In addition, kids who wanted to were more than welcome to play poker but again the

House got a percentage of every pot. Basically, the House won every time.

We actually never allowed anyone to drink our parents' alcohol but we were gracious hosts providing beverages and snacks. Again nothing was free but we didn't gouge on our prices either so our happy clients returned day after day to play pool, poker and just hang out.

Of course there are many other stories to tell about childhood but there isn't enough time or paper to tell them all. Suffice it to say, my siblings and I learned self sufficiency and we developed a strong bond between the five of us. Over our lifetimes we have always remained close and I believe our many adventures as children helped to form that strong bond of family that has always been one of the most important things in all of our lives.

Chapter Three – Teen Age Events

This is going to be one of the shortest chapters. My teenage years were nothing to be excited about. I was a shy quiet geek of a teenager. I wasn't really involved in anything while in high school. In fact if you look at my high school yearbook, each year I am listed on one page and only one page.

I sucked at sports and athletics. In fact my high school required each student to take so many classes of phys ed (gym) but I sucked so bad that my high school gym teacher didn't even want to teach me. So instead, he made me the Locker room monitor. During gym class, I never had to get changed into gym clothes and I didn't have to participate. I just sat in his office doing my homework and I made sure that nobody stole anything out of the locker room. It worked for him and it worked for me.

I set one goal for myself when I started high school and I am proud to say that I achieved that goal. My goal was to never take home a book to study but yet I wanted to graduate in the top 10% of my class. Well I never took home a book and I never studied at home – just in study hall – and I graduated number 30 in a class of 330! So not bad! (According to legal counsel, I am now obligated to state "If there are any kids reading this please don't try this at home".)

The biggest and most important event of my teenage years was when I accidentally enlisted in the Army Reserves my junior year of high school at the age of 17. Yes, I accidentally enlisted. Here is what happened.

It was Christmas break 1982 and somehow I managed to enlist myself in the United States Army Reserves. I hadn't planned on it in fact as I stated above in the Ancestor Chapter, there was a time and argument between my father and I where my father had told me that I needed to join the military so that "they could make a man out of me" and I had informed him that I "would NEVER be in the military". I guess the lesson to be learned is "never say never!"

Here is what happened. My oldest sister had graduated from high school in 1981 and by Christmas of 1982, she still hadn't found her way in the post-high school world. She had decided to investigate the United States Army. So one afternoon, her Army recruiter was at our home talking to her and my parents about what was necessary to enter the Army and what great benefits she would get just by joining the Army.

My sister decided that she wanted to give it a chance. When she asked the recruiter what the next step would be he stated that she needed to take the Military Aptitude test. This man went on to describe how difficult the aptitude test was because of how important a potential enlistee's score was from the test. He told stories about what kind of score an enlistee would need for certain types of jobs and what was an average score.

As I sat there listening, I couldn't help but think that it couldn't be that hard of a test because I always thought that the military pretty much took anyone who was breathing and was able to sign their name on the dotted line. Also, school had always come easy for me and so I spouted off about the fact that the test couldn't be all that hard.

The recruiter then turned to me and began a conversation that went like this:

RECRUITER: "How old are you son?"
ME: "17"
RECRUITER: "Have you ever thought about enlisting in the military?"
ME: "NO – I am going to college; I have no desire to join the military"
RECRUITER: "How are you going to pay for college?"
ME: "I don't know"
RECRUITER: "The military could help pay for it."
ME: "I am not joining the military"
ME: "Besides, I am not old enough to join and I don't graduate from high school until 1984"
RECRUITER: "You can join the Reserves now while you are 17. You go to basic training this summer between your junior year and senior year. Then after you graduate from high school, you go to your advance training. In between you go to weekend meetings at your Reserve center once a month. In addition, you spend two weeks each summer at an Annual Training to enhance your military skills."

ME: "I don't think I want to spend my summer vacation at Army basic training."
RECRUITER: "Oh well, you probably couldn't pass the test"
ME": "I could pass the test without even trying!"
RECRUITER: "Easy for you to say when you aren't willing to take it and prove yourself. However, if you want to prove yourself, you can come down to the recruiting office and take it with your sister tomorrow."
ME: "I don't think so."
RECRUITER: "I understand you are afraid you can't pass it."
ME: "No, I am not afraid that I can't pass it I just don't want to take it"
RECRUITER: "Ok Mr. Chicken its ok maybe in a year you won't be so afraid and you can take the test then."
ME: "I AM NOT AFRAID"
RECRUITER: "OK then take the test!"
ME: "OK – I'll show you!"

So basically, I was goaded into taking the test. At the time, I kept saying, "I am not joining, I am not joining."

The next day, the recruiter showed up and I and my parents filled out tons of paperwork which I thought was a waste of time because I was just taking the test to show the recruiter how smart I was. However, as always you can't do anything involving the government without the paperwork so we signed the paperwork. Once all of the letter I's had been dotted and the letter T's had been crossed and the forms were signed, my sister, I and the recruiter headed off to the test.

The test was in my opinion a piece of cake. Afterwards, the recruiter informed me that I had scored high enough to select any job within the US Army that I wanted. (I will admit that I don't know if that was the whole truth and nothing but the truth about this issue – I never saw my test scores and to this day, I am not sure what I scored but I will take the recruiter's word for it that I scored that well. In addition, I don't remember if we received our scores that day or if we had to wait for the scores to come back.)

Oh yeah, my sister passed the test as well.

The next time the recruiter met with my sister, my parents and me, it was to tell us that the next step was to take a Medical Physical up in Cleveland. At this point my sister said ok schedule a physical for her and I said, that I wasn't interested. However, my mother said that it wouldn't hurt to take the physical and see what job they could offer me in the reserves. She also had this great idea (thanks to Mr. Recruiter (the man who would have lied and sold his own mother into slavery to get a new recruit on the books)) that maybe the job that the Army would offer me would have a bonus attached and it would help pay for college. So, I was talked into going to Cleveland to take the physical exam. After all as my mother kept saying "it couldn't hurt to hear what the Army would offer" and at this point all the paperwork was signed including my parents' permission so why waste all that great government paperwork that was done in triplicate.

The physicals were scheduled for January 3, 1983 – which was to be the first day back to school after Xmas break but my mom and dad gave me permission to miss school on the third of January (bless their hearts). On, January 2, 1983, when the recruiter came to pick my sister and myself up, my sister chickened out. I think I really wanted to chicken out too, however, I was too stubborn and to proud to chicken out. So, the recruiter took me down to the bus station in downtown Canton. He put me on a Greyhound bus bound for Cleveland and I was on my way. At this point in my life, I had never been away from home on my own ever.

When I arrived in Cleveland, there was a person from the military that herded us to the Cleveland Holiday Inn and checked us into the hotel. I was assigned to a room with a perfect stranger. This was my first time ever to stay in a hotel without my family and I was supposed to sleep in a room with a total stranger. What an Army!

The guy that was assigned to my room was 21 and was leaving the next day for the Navy. We were told that we were to stay in the rooms but he was like "NOT ME." He had one night left as a civilian and he was going out on the town and he left. I never saw him again. I have often wondered since then over these many years if he ever made it to Navy boot camp the next day or if he just took off and never left for Boot Camp.

On the morning of January 3, 1983, every potential enlistee that was staying at the Holiday Inn were awakened bright and early, shepherded onto a bus and driven over to the Federal Building to the MEPS (Military Enlistment Processing Station – I think). We were then led into the cafeteria, fed breakfast then taken up to the MEPS floor of the Federal Building. At the MEP station that day, we began by filling in more paperwork then we were led through various stations. There were eye exams, hearing exams, etc. before being led into a room and being told to strip down to our underwear and there we were two lines of men standing around in our underwear. Next, one very old doctor (I think he delivered Adam back in the day) entered the room and walked down the line listening to everyone's heart etc. Then we had to drop our underwear and there we stood two lines of butt ass naked men of all races, sizes, shapes and ages looking at each other as this doctor walked down the line grabbing hold of everyone and saying "Turn your head and cough!" After this delightful activity we were ordered to do an about face so the two lines were facing away from each other and we then were ordered to bend over. At this point the doctor made his way down the line of naked bent over men checking out our posteriors. At this point, I was screaming in my head "WHY AM I F#$#$#$# HERE?" However, I did learn that day that in the Army's eyes all enlisted men are treated "equally" regardless of race.

Following that adventure we were provided the customary cups to fill with urine specimens. We filled the cups as an observer sat on a stool and watched us pee into the cups. Again as a 17 year old kid from a little town, I just thought to myself "they pay this guy to watch other guys pee into these tiny cups – isn't America great!"

After the viewing of the piss, it was then onto the room where each potential enlistee was fingerprinted and then they were sent onto the Question and Answer section of the exam.

Have you ever engaged in Homosexual Sex?
Have you ever used illegal drugs?
Have you ever been convicted of a felony?
Do you currently wet the bed?
Etc

Of course, I might have the order of that day's events somewhat out of order due to the fact that it has been 82 years and the fact that so much of it was bizarre but you get the gist of what happened. In addition, in between the various stations, there was a lot of hurrying up and waiting that was typical of the U.S. Military with some yelling and screaming done by the workers thrown in for extra measure.

Finally after they were fully satisfied that my body was sound and that I could survive the rigors of basic training and they were assured based on my answers that I wasn't a homosexual (which they feared would destroy good order and discipline), a drug using criminal or some combination thereof and the fact that I was either dumb enough or willing to go through all this, that I could progress to the final two steps of the day.

Final Step #1 – Select a military job. This is the step where the enlistee met with a "Career Counselor" and would find out what jobs they were eligible for. Now my list was somewhat shorter because I was joining the reserves and not active duty but the counselor said that it was going to be easy to find me a job because of my (supposedly incredibly high) scores. He asked me what Reserve unit I wanted to join and I said I wanted to join the one that was the closest to my home. There were three units at that time that were about the same distance from my home. An MP (Military Police) unit in North Canton, a Transportation Unit (truck drivers) in Canton or a military hospital in Canton. As soon as he said the three units, I knew I didn't want to be an MP or a truck driver so I chose the military hospital. I didn't have a clue what all it meant to join a military hospital but he said it was like the television series MASH (a great show that if you have never seen, you should get it on DVD and watch it).

So the counselor said ok if you want to join the military hospital, you can do one of the following jobs there because these are the openings they currently have. (Just a side note, he was checking this all in a book that was on his desk because at this time there wasn't a computer on his desk.)

Anyway here are the choices he gave me:

Ambulance Driver – wasn't sure I wanted to go down that road.
Lab Technician – sounded too much like chemistry – yuck!
X-Ray Technician – I didn't see much developing there.
OR Technician – this intrigued me mostly because I had no idea what it was.

So, I asked what an OR Tech was and the guy says "you get to go into surgery and assist the surgeon, passing him instruments, holding instruments and etc." I was thinking that would be cool. The counselor then asked if I had problems with seeing blood and I said, no. I didn't know if I did or I didn't but I figured I could deal with it when I had to, so I said no. The counselor then informed me that I would get a $ 5,000 bonus if I enlisted for that job. At the age of 17, $ 5,000 sounded like a huge fortune.

Of course, I still thought that I wasn't going to join the military. In fact, at this point, I thought that we would talk jobs and then I would get to go home and talk to my parents and think about it. However, this is where my accidental enlistment happened. The counselor filled out all of the paperwork and had me sign all sorts of papers (which I didn't read) and then I was led into the next room which would be Final Step #2.

The next thing I knew this guy comes in and says "Raise your right hand and repeat after me…

The Oath of Enlistment (for enlistees):

"I, Jay B .Barton, do solemnly swear (or affirm) that I will support and defend the Constitution of the United States against all enemies, foreign and domestic; that I will bear true faith and allegiance to the same; and that I will obey the orders of the President of the United States and the orders of the officers appointed over me, according to regulations and the Uniform Code of Military Justice. So help me God."

And there it was, I had accidentally sworn to support and defend the Constitution and I had enlisted in the United States Army Reserves. At that point in my life I didn't have the wherewithal to protest and I just swore that oath.

The next day, I returned to Louisville High School and the second half of my junior year in high school.

I guess you could say that my "accidental enlistment" pretty much sums up my teenage years from age 13 to 17. I was just there for my teenage years not an active participant just a participant.

However, my final two teenage years, were dramatically different thanks to the summer between my junior year and senior year of high school.

Basic Training

I finished my junior year in high school the last week of May 1983. Within the next week, I had my Senior Pictures taken and my family and friends threw me a "Going Away Party" and I left the comfort of being a teenage boy living at home to become a man.

The second week of June, 1983, I was once again put on a Greyhound bus in Canton, Ohio and sent to Cleveland, Ohio. Upon arrival at Cleveland, I was taken to that same Holiday Inn and this time, I was not assigned a roommate. I don't remember sleeping too much because it was after I arrived in the room that I finally started thinking about the fact that I was headed for Army Basic Training. For the next 8 weeks of my life I was going to be a soldier with an in your face hard core Drill Sergeant controlling my life. Think about some of the movies that you have seen over the years that included scenes about basic training. Now imagine being 17 years old and this is how you were going to spend your summer. Talk about asking yourself; WHAT WAS I THINKING?!!!!

I don't really remember sleeping much. I kept wondering what Fort McClellan, Alabama was going to be like. I was hoping that I would be assigned to the same group that some guys I had met at my reserve unit in Canton (I had been required to attend a few meetings before going to basic training – I will talk more about this in another chapter) were going to be in at Fort McClellan. They had left a few days before me and they were headed to Fort McClellan too.

The next morning, I had to go through a shortened version of the fun filled first day when I had gone up to Cleveland in January of 1983. A doctor checked out my vitals and I was asked the questions about drugs, my sexual behavior and if I had committed any crimes since the last time I had been there. Then they sent me into a room to wait with the other enlistees that were being "shipped out that day".

At some point they came into the room and called out all the guys leaving for the Navy, then the Marines and the Air Force. Finally, they came in and started calling out groups for the Army. The first group was guys going to Fort McClellan and my name wasn't on the list. I went up to the guy who was calling out the names to inquire as to why I wasn't on the Fort McClellan list and he ORDERED me to wait for my name to be called. WOW my first military order – and I started thinking I was in trouble.

Finally, I was the last person called and I was in a group by myself. The guy who barked at me earlier who was just a PFC but to me at that moment could have been a General since I really didn't know ranks said "there has been a change you are going to Fort Dix". I had no clue where that was and I asked if my parents would be notified. His answer was "they will find out when the Army wants them to know. Take your tickets and your directions – go get on the van, it will take you to the Airport, check in at this counter, and get on this flight."

So I went and got in the van and went to Cleveland Hopkins airport. I had never been on a plane before and didn't know the first thing about airports. Luckily there were people from the military at the airport who directed me in the right way. In reality I think they did it to make sure I (or any other recruit) didn't run away. I was put onto a late afternoon flight for Baltimore, Maryland – I still didn't know where Fort Dix was at this point. The flight landed in Baltimore and then I had to get on a flight for Philadelphia, Pennsylvania. When I landed in Philly, I had to find the Military desk and when I got there, I was put into a room with a bunch of other guys headed to Fort Dix. At about midnight we were loaded onto a bus and off we went to Fort Dix. On the way in, I finally saw a sign that indicated that we were in New Jersey.

Upon arrival at Fort Dix, I was getting more and more scared. I kept expecting the Drill Sergeant to jump on the bus and to start yelling and screaming and pushing us off the bus just like in the movies. However, when we finally arrived none of that happened. We were led to a cafeteria, fed and then led to a dorm to sleep. I barely remembered sleeping and we were being woke up again. Again we were ordered to fall in and things didn't seem so bad. No real yelling etc. I was totally disoriented and at a total loss. We were led thru the Reception Station. We filled out more forms, we received our shots (as in vaccinations not shots of tequila), we began to learn the basics of military customs and courtesies, and of course we had our hair shaved off. Finally, as I was beginning to think that basic wasn't going to be all that bad, someone pointed out to me this wasn't basic training and these guys weren't Drill Sergeants. I was so naïve and unprepared for what was happening to me. At the end of the first week it finally dawned on me – this past week doesn't count – I was going to be gone from home for 9 weeks not 8.

Oh yeah – at some point in time I was given the opportunity to call home and let my parents know that I was in New Jersey and not Alabama – surprise!

Well finally after the Reception Station week it came time to go to my basic training platoon. We were loaded up onto the "Cattle Cars" and driven to the basic training area. The cattle cars were given that name because they were trailers that looked like the trailers used to haul cows in the real world. In basic training they were the trailers that we the trainees were loaded onto when we were lucky enough not to have to march.

When we arrived at the basic training area, this is where the Drill Sergeants of my nightmares came to life. Yelling! Screaming! Hollering! Name calling! "GET YOUR ASSES OFF MY CATTLE CAR YOU WORTHLESS MAGGOTS!" All of the movie clichés – we heard them all.

"I AM YOUR MOMMA and YOUR DADDY FOR THE NEXT 8 WEEKS – YOU DON'T DO ANYTHING WITHOUT MY PERMISSION YOU DON'T EVEN SHIT UNLESS I TELL YOU TO SHIT."

"DO YOU UNDERSTAND ME? Yes sir! DON'T CALL ME SIR – I AM AN NCO, I WORK FOR A LIVING – IT IS YES DRILL SGT" Yes drill sgt.

"I CANT HEAR YOU". Then we would yell louder then the Drill Sgt and scream – YES DRILL SGT.

On and on and on it went.

At this point things became just a blur.

In time we were taught how to store our gear in our lockers.

We were taught what was expected of us every morning – cleaning the barracks, making our beds, shining our boots.

We were taught how to wear our uniforms.

We were assigned to KP (Kitchen Police), door guards, CQ Runner etc.

We were told when we would have free time (rarely if ever).

We were made to do pushups and do lots of running.

I was made a road guard. This meant that whenever we had to march, I had to wear an orange safety vest and whenever our platoon came to a road, the Drill Sergeant would yell "ROAD GUARDS POST" and we would have to run ahead of the platoon and stand in the middle of the street and stop traffic. Then after the platoon had crossed the street, the Drill Sergeant would yell "ROAD GUARDS RECOVER" and we would have to run back to the platoon and get back into our position. I wasn't assigned this job because the Drill Sergeant liked me but rather I was assigned this to make me do some extra running because I was one of the slowest and worst at running in the platoon.

So, the days blurred together. Wake up, get yelled at, eat breakfast get yelled at, march here or there, get yelled at, do pushups, do Physical Training, get yelled at, do more pushups, learn more marching, get yelled at, more pushups, eat lunch, learn more military customs and laws, get yelled at, do more pushups, march some more, get yelled at, learn more stuff, eat dinner, get yelled at, march some more, more pushups, clean the barracks, and finally go to bed. Over and over.

At first I seemed so out of it and that I was never going to catch on but I did. I managed to learn how to march, how to salute, I learned my three general orders, I could identify all the Army ranks, I knew when to salute and when not to salute, I was able to do enough pushups and enough situps and run the 2 miles in the right amount of time etc.

I had even survived the GAS CHAMBER. The Gas Chamber was a wonderful right of passage in basic training. The recruits were taken into a building where the Drill Sergeants had tear gas waiting. We were ordered to put on our Protective masks and the tear gas was let loose. Then we were ordered to remove the protective masks and inhale the tear gas. If you have never experienced it – it is a nasty experience. The Drill Sergeants then asked each recruit questions and you had to answer them which forced you to breathe in more of the gas. The questions continued until they finally decided that you were sufficiently tortured and they would let you out of the building. Then you had to go outside and run in circles hoping to get the stuff off your body. Your eyes would be burning and running, you had snot running out of your nose and you just wanted to die. Yeah it was real pleasant! Then after this wonderful experience we were forced marched to a bivouac site (campsite for civilians). Of course summer in New Jersey is hot and humid so the more you sweat the more the Tear Gas comes out of your clothes and pores and before long as we marched along we were being gassed all over again by ourselves. Once we arrived at our bivouac site, we were given a shower to get the gas off our bodies, but of course it was a nice cold shower!

After we returned from this bivouac experience one of the recruits in my platoon decided that he had had enough of the military life. On a Sunday morning, he informed all of us that he was leaving. We didn't believe this guy but then he went down the stairs and out of the front door of our building. He stepped into a taxi that he had called and he just left. Someone decided to go report this to the Drill Sergeant who was on duty and who immediately went ballistic. By the time the Drill Sergeant notified the higher ups and the Fort Dix Military Police, the recruit was already AWOL (Absent With Out Leave) and was already out the front gate.

The AWOL had the cab driver drive him to the bus station and he purchased a ticket to take him home. The guy bought a ticket straight to his home town so it wasn't hard for the Military Police to track him down and apprehend him. When his bus arrived in his home town the MPs were waiting for him. He was immediately arrested and returned to Fort Dix, NJ. They brought him back and stood him in front of our barracks for 12 hours. They forced him to stand there in his shackles (wrists and ankles) so that the rest of us got the message that going AWOL was not acceptable. The message was received.

The next phase of our training was when we were issued our M-16s and started going to the firing range. This was my downfall. I could barely hit the broad side of a barn and I failed to qualify with my M-16 and I ended up being recycled. Recycled meant that I was sent to another platoon and it meant two more weeks in basic training and returning home with only one week before my senior year would start. Absolutely no summer break for me.

Luckily, when I got recycled one of my new drill sergeants was able to teach me how to fire the M-16 successfully and to pass my basic rifle course with an expert marksmanship award. He realized that while I was not able to shoot right handed like I write, I could shoot anything left handed. Thank God for him or I might still be at Ft. Dix, New Jersey as a recruit to this day.

During basic training, every recruit was paired with a "buddy". Buddies were supposed to be there for each other and help each other survive the Basic Training experience. When I got recycled I was assigned as a buddy to an African American recruit. My buddy's name was Pvt. Wales. Thank God I was assigned to him for a multitude of reasons. He became one of the best friends I have ever known. Most guys would not have been happy being assigned a recycled troop who couldn't hang with his original platoon. However, he was great and the moment we met he said he was going to make sure I made it out of Basic Training with him.

Aside from our racial differences, another amazing thing about this situation was that he & I couldn't have been more different. I was the youngest recruit (17) in our platoon and I had grown up in a small Ohio town that was 100% white and he was the oldest recruit in our platoon (25) and he had grown up in a very poor and very tough section of Los Angeles, CA that was 100% African American. We had some great conversations during the weeks I was with him at Basic Training. I told him about where I had been raised and how and he was shocked at first that he was the first African American I had ever really gotten to know but he asked me if I believed what I had been told about race issues or whether I had a different opinion. I told him that since I had joined the Army, I was beginning to see that everything I had ever known about race relations was so wrong and that I was glad that I had gotten to know him. He just looked at me and said you are ok kid and then he went on to say "besides growing up I never saw any white boys in my neighborhood so I imagine the things I grew up hearing about whites was just as bad and at times just as untrue." We remained in contact through phone calls and letters over the years after basic training. Unlike me he was a member of the Active Duty Army and so after basic he went to Combat Medic school and went on and was stationed in Germany. He was promoted eventually to Command Sgt Major and died of cancer following Desert Storm. Like I said he was one of my best friends ever and I still miss him.

But back to Basic Training . . . .

At my new platoon, I sort of came face to face with the meanest baddest, most foul mouthed drill sergeant I ever saw at Ft. Dix, New Jersey. In fact, this drill sergeant has to have been the meanest one in the entire history of the United States Army. Now the reason, that I said that I sort of came face to face with the drill sergeant was because she only stood five feet tall. Yes the ultimate nightmare drill sergeant was a WOMAN.

Staff Sergeant Branderson could out run, out cuss and out do every male Drill Sergeant at Fort Dix. This woman (I always assumed she was a woman but perhaps she was a genetic mutation), seemed to love to march us across Fort Dix singing cadence just so she could say the "F" word.

Her favorite cadence while marching us was the Little Bird. It went like this:

Drill Sgt: "A little bird"
Platoon: "A little bird"
Drill Sgt: "with a yellow bill"
Platoon: "with a yellow bill"
Drill Sgt: "was perched upon"
Platoon: "was perched upon"
Drill Sgt: "my window sill"
Platoon: "my window sill"
Drill Sgt: "I lured him in"
Platoon: "I lured him in"
Drill Sgt: "with crumbs of bread"
Platoon: "with crumbs of bread"
Drill Sgt: "and then I crushed"
Platoon: "and then I crushed"
Drill Sgt: "his **FUCKING** Head"
Platoon: "his fucking head"

Over and over she would sing that with the F word emphatically repeated each and every time. She sang the F word no matter where we were on the post even in front of the post chapel on Sunday mornings. As I remember it that is the only cadence she ever sang as she marched us. The words would only be interrupted if as she sang she had to spit! Yes I said spit because she chewed tobacco.

Other things I remember about this woman was that because she was so short every member of our platoon looked over her head. She would be in front of a soldier yelling and screaming and then she would ask "why aren't you looking at me while I am talking to you?" The recruit would immediately look down to make eye contact and then she would scream "your eyes are supposed to be straight ahead when you are at the position of attention." It was a no win situation.

Towards the end of basic training she informed our platoon that if our parents and loved ones were coming to watch our graduation, she would make sure we got to see our loved ones the night before graduation. So, after our graduation practice, she marched us back to our barracks and there across the street were my parents and siblings. I went up to Drill Sergeant Branderson and told her that my family was across the street and I requested permission to go see them. She said "NO" and I protested and reminded her that she had said that if our parents were in town the day before we would get to see them. She looked up at me and said "I didn't lie – there are your parents and you "SEE" them right recruit?" She of course was right. She didn't actually say that we would get to talk to them or be next to them – just see them. Eventually after more families showed up she let us cross the street to go see our loved ones. She even eventually allowed us to go with them and spend that last night of basic training with our families in their motel rooms. I guess she did have a heart or some portion thereof.

What I learned in basic training were some of the greatest life lessons I could ever learn. I learned that I was tougher than I thought. I learned to judge my fellow men on who they are and by their actions and not by the color of their skin. I also found self confidence in myself and my abilities.

After graduation from Basic Training, my parents, my siblings and I left Fort Dix, New Jersey and we headed for home. About an hour from the Ohio border there was a huge accident on the Pennsylvania Turnpike and we ended up sitting on the turnpike for about 6 hours. It was hot and nasty. No food! No air conditioning because everyone shut down their vehicles! It was great because I was no longer on Fort Dix and I was free.

Eventually we made it home and I returned to my senior year in high school. It was weird returning to high school for many reasons. The biggest was the fact that for the entire summer I had been treated like an adult but then I was back in high school and I was expected to be a teenager. I remember having a new attitude and at times it was good and at times it wasn't. I really didn't care about the "kid stuff" that my classmates cared about. I remember in my senior government class we were having a discussion about the legal drinking age. At about that time, the Federal Government was mandating that the drinking age be raised to 21 in every state or the states wouldn't receive Federal Highway money for repairs. Ohio had been a state that had allowed 18 year olds to drink 3.2 Beer (just lower alcohol content) and of course my classmates were angry that now that we were turning 18 that the age limit had been raised right out from under us. One girl stood up and said that it wasn't fair because if somebody was old enough to serve in the military then he or she should be old enough to drink. I chimed in "if you serve in the military you can drink on base at 18. In fact you can drink at 17 because I did it this summer." Everyone turned to look at me like I didn't know what I was talking about. So, I told them that I had spent my summer in Basic Training and that we were given a Saturday night off at the end of our training and that I had been served alcohol at the NCO club. I hadn't told anyone that I was going to basic training that summer and nobody believed what I was saying about it. The teacher (a weasel of a woman) even told me to stop telling fibs or she would give me detention. I looked at her and said "I am not lying and I will give you prove because right here is my military ID and if you want I will bring my paperwork from basic training and show you."

The weasel's response was "ok that's two weeks detention and you can go to the Vice Principal's office right now!"

I looked at her and I couldn't believe it. I stood up and told her "you are going to regret that decision and you won't be here on Monday!" As I walked out of her classroom I slammed the door. I walked down to the Vice Principal's office and told him why I was there and that the teacher had called me a liar.

His response was "you weren't really in basic training this summer!"

So, I told him to call my mother at work which he did. As he hung up the phone he apologized to me and told me that he would talk to the Weasel and that he would fix it.

My response was that he needed to call her down right now and make her apologize to my face and then she owed me another apology in front of the class. He wasn't sure that he could make that happen so I looked him square in the eye and said either he did or my story would be all over the newspaper the next day. I said I can see it now "Soldier called a liar by a high school teacher!" I told him I was sure that the newspaper would love a human interest story about a young 17 year old patriotic kid going through basic training and completing such a significant event only to come back to high school for his senior year and be called a LIAR by a misinformed arrogant school teacher.

The Vice Principal called the teacher down to his office. When she walked in she told him that I had been disrespectful etc. He told her to apologize to me because I had in fact completed Army

Basic Training that summer. The Weasel refused! So we had a little stand off and so I asked the Vice Principal to excuse me from school for the rest of the day because I had to get a hold of the newspaper or maybe since it was government class, I could also call my congressman. He refused.

However to his credit he told me to return to the classroom and that he was going to call in the principal. In the end, the School Superintendent was called in. The next morning, the Weasel of a teacher apologized to me in front of our Senior Government class and immediately thereafter she was gone for a two week suspension.

When she returned from her suspension she still had it in for me. She even went so far to give me an "F" on a test that I had actually gotten an "A" on. However, I stood up for myself throughout the whole ordeal and eventually, I was removed from her class and put into the other Senior Government class taught by another teacher. In the end that ended up being her last year teaching at my high school.

Prior to Army Basic Training, I would have never stood up for myself and so yes during Basic Training, I found my spine or my voice or whatever you want to call it and I never lost my voice after that.

Chapter Four – Army & College

AIT / OJT

AIT was my Advanced Individual Training for the Military. I did it the summer and fall after I graduated from High School. Now normally, a soldier goes straight from Basic Training to AIT but not me. I was a Split Training Soldier so that added a special something to the experience. I was put back into that military training mode after basically having been a civilian for a year. I was thrown back into the mix with all of the gung ho basic training Rambo graduates. However, in short order, I got right back into it.

The first part of my AIT took place at Ft. Sam Houston which is in San Antonio, TX. First of all let me put an end to one of those old myths about Texas heat vs. Ohio heat. There are certain people who love to say that 112 degrees Fahrenheit in Texas isn't as hot as 112 in Ohio because Texas heat is a "DRY HEAT". Let me tell you they have never been there. Dry heat or humid heat, Texas is as hot as Ohio and as hot as the place that I hope I don't end up going to when I die.

So after acclimating to the summer heat of Texas and being back on active duty in the military, I really enjoyed my summer in Texas and my AIT. Now my military occupational specialty (MOS) was an Operating Room Technician and so here is what my training consisted of:

A. 8 weeks of Combat Medic School – similar to an EMT.
   1. We learned first aid
   2. We learned CPR
   3. We learned how to take vitals
   4. We learned how to give shots
   5. We learned how to take blood
   6. We learned how to start IVs
   7. We learned basic anatomy & physiology

B. 8 weeks of OR Tech School – classroom setting
   1. We learned more Anatomy & Physiology
   2. We learned Medical Terminology
   3. We learned all of the surgical instruments
   4. We learned all of the surgical equipment
   5. We learned about sutures
   6. We learned how to pass instruments to the surgeon

7. We learned how to gown & glove
8. We learned how to scrub for surgery
9. We learned OR procedures

C. 10 weeks of OJT (On the Job Training) working in an actual Operating Room in an actual military hospital.

That's the technical side of what my AIT was about. The real side was it was basically a huge adventure for me and I loved almost every minute of it. It was my second time away from home and this time I wasn't on lock down like I had been when I was at Ft. Dix, New Jersey the summer before for Basic Training.

San Antonio is a great city and I saw as much of it as possible while I was there. The River Walk, The Alamo, (both the real one which seems so small and the one that was used in all the westerns which is much larger than the actual one), the San Antonio Zoo, and so much more.

I also learned about drinking that summer. While the drinking laws back then said that you had to be 21 to drink alcohol, I was served alcohol anytime I wanted in San Antonio on the River Walk if I was wearing my uniform. In addition, at that time, on military bases, it was still legal to drink at the age of 18 at the NCO club on base. My drinks of choice back then were beer or Whiskey Sours. Not that that matters but I just thought that I would throw it out there.

There were several interesting things that happened during my time in AIT. During the first 8 weeks when we were going through the Combat Medic portion of our training, we were in a more Basic Training Mode. This meant that we were marched as a platoon from place to place while on duty. During our off time we were always required to be in uniform and we weren't allowed to wear civilian clothes, and we had an NCO that was like a drill sergeant from basic training. Lots of yelling and hollering and he was in total control of our lives. One of those NCOs was a Staff Sergeant Williams and he thought he was Mr. Cool. He was basically an ok guy the majority of time but he could also be a real prick. He especially loved being a prick about our uniforms. His was always freshly starched and pressed each day and his boots were as shiny as any boots that I had ever seen. He was definitely a squared away trooper on the surface. However, in addition to being a prick at times he was a pervert. The man's favorite pastime during our classroom breaks was to have our platoon sit in a circle and then he would ask for volunteers to get up and tell sex stories or even worse he would tell about his latest and greatest sexual conquest. Obviously, this was prior to any real Sexual Harassment policies being in place and/or being taken seriously in the military.

However, about our fourth week into training he was relieved of duty and we never saw him again. We were to have PT (physical training) and when we all fell out into formation we were wearing our gym shorts and t-shirts. At the time the Army had a regulation that required female soldiers to wear bras at all time. However, one female troop decided to show up into PT formation wearing shorts, shirt and no bra. Well, Staff Sergeant Williams took notice that she was lacking the proper support and so he got up in her face and asked her "Soldier are you wearing a bra?" Her answer was "yes Staff Sergeant Williams". He repeated his question and basically called this female out as a liar. When she yet again repeated that yes she was wearing a bra, he ordered her to come stand in front of the platoon and to lift her hands and arms above her head as he stood behind her. When the young woman did this he grabbed a hold of her t-shirt and pulled it up and off of her. Of course he was right that she wasn't wearing a bra and there she stood in front of the whole platoon topless. She was extremely embarrassed and she ran off as our whole platoon just stood there stunned. After that stunt Staff Sergeant Williams was gone.

After being separated into male & female training units for basic training, suddenly all the young men & women were brought back together and suddenly we were spending a lot of time together. Even though we were segregated in Male & Female Dormitories, there was a whole lot of sex going on (not to mention the pervert NCO that I talked about above who asked soldiers for sex stories or shared his own). I will admit right now that my sexual life has always been very conservative but more than 50% (and I truly think the number is a lot higher) of the members of the Army that I have seen are nothing but sex maniacs (both male and female versions) (read later story "Summer Camp Wives"). Most of the sex happened on weekends off when we were allowed to leave the base and we weren't required to be back until Monday morning. Most troops that were hooking up would get a cheap hotel room and do their thing. However, by the end of the month most troops had very little money left over because back in the day the military didn't do much to help the young troops learn about finances so, soldiers were rich at the first of the month and living off government assistance at the end of the month (eating in the mess hall not at McDonalds).

Well when horny people get horny they get creative in how they decide to scratch that itch. The worst story of being creative was when one couple decided to do it inside a dumpster – yes a trash dumpster. I was on fireguard (when on fireguard duty at Ft. Sam for the Combat medic portion of the training, you stood at the door on the ground floor to make sure that only the authorized people went upstairs to the dorms and that nothing funny went on in the area around the building) on a Friday night at about 11:00pm when the NCO in charge came out to check on myself and the other fireguard, we made the discovery that is burned into my mind forever.

We heard a lot of moaning and groaning and screaming coming from the trash dumpster. So, I, the other fireguard and the NCO walk over to the dumpster and we opened it up and as we shined our flashlights into it we were startled to discover the happy couple on top of the trash doing "it"!

They were shocked! We were shocked! The NCO started screaming and the couple was trying to get their clothes on and to get out of the dumpster. However, the NCO decided something else was more appropriate. He ordered them to throw out their clothes. Of course as he was yelling a crowd grew around the dumpster and people were hooting and hollering. Finally after he had lectured the Happy Trash Sex Couple, he decided to let them get out of the dumpster and off they ran to their respective dorms butt assed naked because he had ordered them to throw out their clothes and he wouldn't return them. On Monday, they were sent back to the beginning of training and the NCO in question became our primary NCO.

The surprising thing was that the following month when money was again short because of the end of the month thing (on the last week of that 8 week stretch of the training) there was another couple caught in the exact same dumpster having sex. Ironically, it was the NCO that had caught the original Trash Sex couple and a male recruit. This meant two discharges since back in the day homosexuals were automatically discharged. As a side note: the "no homosexuals in the military policy" was always a joke. I knew several excellent soldiers over the years who served and who also just happened to be gay. They served and they served honorably and they were great at their jobs yet had anyone known they would have been booted. Ironically in the above story the original "Trash Sex" couple faced absolutely no discipline for their actions but the same sex couple was booted. When I became President, I dropped "Don't Ask / Don't Tell" and ordered that gays be allowed to serve in the military.

Following the combat medic portion of my training, I went up the hill (as they used to call it) at Ft. Sam to the portion that seemed much more like college. We had nicer accommodations to live in. We were allowed to wear our civilian clothes on our off duty hours and we came and went as we pleased. The only rule was that we weren't allowed to miss class and we weren't allowed to be late. We did still have to pull fireguard duty at our buildings but that was it.

The OR Tech School was basically one big party. We hung out and drank and just had fun until "they" moved into the buildings behind us. "They" were some Special Forces Soldiers who were at Ft. Sam to learn Medic skills. Special Force Soldiers were required to learn life saving skills because of the type of missions they carried out. When they were on clandestine missions, they weren't always allowed to call in a medic to save them so they were all trained as medics so that they could provide their own medical services in an emergency. Part of their training included being on a field exercise that involved their instructors shooting a live pig and the Special Force troops had to keep the pig alive for so many hours or they would fail their course. These guys were hard core troops and they had already completed the Special Forces courses where they were trained to kill. They were very GUNG HO bad asses.

Well after they arrived for their training and took up residence behind our buildings, they decided that I and my classmates were no longer allowed to hang out in the green space between the buildings. In addition, we weren't allowed to use the picnic tables that were in the green space even though there were enough for all of us to use. So, after our banishment, we all got together and decided it was time to take a stand. We turned to one of our classmates for guidance. This soldier was the oldest in our group and he was changing his MOS (Military Occupational Skill) after having been a Combat Infantry man for almost 18 years. The guy had seen action in combat in Vietnam. He was the real deal and more of a soldier than the Special Forces that were giving us trouble.

He decided that what we would do was paint the picnic tables HOT PINK. So we all chipped in and we bought several gallons of Pink paint at a hardware store and in the middle of the night we painted every picnic table a very lovely shade of pink. We all went to bed at about 4:00am and we had to be ready for PT (physical training – exercise) at 6:00am. When we got into formation for PT we were tired but we were very proud of our accomplishments. All of the females in our unit showed up for PT that morning wearing pink shorts and pink shirts. Well, the Special Forces soldiers weren't so happy when they woke and saw the pink picnic tables and their commanding officer immediately came to our side of the buildings to get to the bottom of the matter. He yelled and screamed and hollered. He demanded to inspect every troop in our class. He wanted to look at everyone's fingers for pink paint. However, there wasn't a drop of pink paint on anyone (we had used surgical gloves taken from class – duh!). He still knew that we had done it because the women were in pink but he couldn't prove anything.

Later that night a couple of the Special Forces Soldiers decided to get their revenge and they started picking on a couple of our classmates. However, our Vietnam Vet interceded and kicked both of the Special Forces Soldiers asses. He took them both on and they didn't put a scratch on him. They both ended up in the hospital. Luckily nothing happened to our Vietnam Vet and the Special Forces Soldiers were moved away and we returned to partying on the picnic tables. They were still pink when I left Fort Sam. A friend of mine later went through the same course at Fort Sam about 2 years later and they were still pink. It was pretty amazing to me that the United States Military never painted them.

After AIT, I and my classmates were shipped to different Army bases all over the country and we were assigned to actually work as OR Techs. I was assigned to Fort Knox, Kentucky. I was sent there with three other students who were all hillbillies from Kentucky. At Fort Knox we were supposed to live on post in the barracks adjacent to the hospital. However, the three hillbillies lived so close to Fort Knox that they all ended up living at home and were never in the barracks. They showed up each day to work but they weren't there for me to hang out with. At first, I ended up working a lot of extra at the hospital because I didn't know anyone and it was something to do. As a result, I got pretty good at my job and I graduated as the top student at OJT. The head OR nurse even tried talking me into staying and going on active duty but I was determined to go home and go to college so I passed on that offer.

After I had been at Ft. Knox for a whole two weeks, I suddenly was thrown into my first solo surgical procedure and it scared me but thrilled me at the same time. I had stuck around after my shift and I was helping the night OR tech prepare for the next day's procedures by pulling all of the necessary equipment and instruments and putting the stuff into each of the OR rooms.

As we worked, an emergency case came into the OR and the overnight tech had to scrub in. So, the on call OR Nurse allowed me to assist her with circulating in the room to gain some experience. But just as the first emergency case began, a second emergency call came in. One of the other OR nurses was still there catching up on paperwork so she volunteered to be in charge of the second emergency surgery. However, they didn't have time to get another real OR tech scrubbed in. So, I was drafted to work the second case. I protested – I claimed "I am just a student." The nurse said don't worry, I will talk you through everything and another tech will be here shortly. You have to do this and do it now.

I scrubbed in and went into the room and got all of the instruments set up. The OR nurse and I performed all the pre surgery counts for the sponges, the blades and the needles. As we finished, the surgeon came in and I had to gown and glove her and then the patient came in. The case was a pregnant woman who needed an emergency C section. I was scared and ready to vomit. The surgeon started and I was in deep you know what. It wasn't even funny but I was surviving and then it happened. A very weird occurrence and it scared me and grossed me out like nothing else has ever done. The baby had been removed and was being attended to by the pediatrician. The surgeon had started to close everything up and things were going great. All of a sudden there was a weird gurgling noise and then all of this blood poured out of this woman over the side and right onto the front of my surgical gown. I could feel it seeping through the gown and seeping through my scrubs. Now this was before AIDS was widely known and at the time surgical personnel didn't wear all of the protection they do now. Luckily, I didn't catch anything. I just wanted out of that room and to get out of my scrubs and to get into a shower. I kept looking at the OR Nurse and she just kept looking at me shaking her head which meant that I wasn't going anywhere. When the other Tech finally got into the room and got gowned and gloved, I counted off all of the sponges, blades, instruments and needles that were on and off the surgical field so fast that the nurse later said I was like a tornado. As I finished the last count, I stepped back from the field and ripped off my surgical gown. I ran out of the door and ran for the showers. I stood in the showers in my scrubs and as the water ran over me, I cut those bloody scrubs off my body with a pair of scissors.

After the C-section from hell, I only scrubbed in one more time as an apprentice. I was soon to be on my own in the OR. The very next morning, I was assigned to work with an experienced OR Tech that was a Staff Sergeant. The case was a knee scope and it was to be a routine slam dunk of a procedure. The only thing was it was with the number one surgeon at Fort Knox. As the Staff Sergeant and I prepped for the case, the Staff Sergeant was being a pompous and arrogant SOB. I couldn't seem to do anything the way he wanted it done. I even managed to piss the guy off when I asked about one of the knife blades being on the handle correctly. They had been having problems where the one type of blade would fall off the handle. We had been instructed to be extremely careful putting them on. I asked the Staff Sergeant "did you double check that the blade was on correctly?" He got angry and he barked at me to just watch and learn. What I did learn that day was a very important lesson which was that pride definitely goes before a fall.

The surgeon came in and he was all business. He said that he just wanted to scope the patients knee and that if he found anything he was sure that he would be able to get it with just a deaver blade (the problem blade) and he would never have to open the knee. The procedure started and the scope was in and everything was going very smoothly. The surgeon even started loosening up. He was asking me questions like where I was from, how old I was and what I planned to do with my life. He then found the problem in the patient's knee and he asked me specifically to hand him the knife with the blade that I had earlier questioned the Staff Sergeant about. As I handed it to him, he asked if the blade was on correctly. I started to say something when the Staff Sergeant, chimed in "Yes sir it is – I put it on the handle myself and I double checked that it was on properly." The surgeon asked if I concurred that the blade was on correctly and I responded that I wasn't sure because when I had asked the Staff Sergeant earlier if he wanted me to double check it, I was ordered to stand back and just observe. The surgeon looked at the Staff Sergeant and said "please check it again." The Staff Sergeant looked at it and said "it's on correctly, I guarantee it!"

The surgeon took the blade and inserted it into the patient's knee and within two seconds the blade was gone and it had fallen off the handle. The surgeon started screaming, cussing and then he got angry. He grabbed a couple of instruments off the table and threw them at the window between the OR and the scrub room and the glass shattered. I was scared and I was shaking. He ordered the Staff Sergeant to get his big dumb ass out of the OR and he looked at me and said "now it's just you and me." The surgeon was determined to find the blade. He looked and looked with the scope but we couldn't find it and yet he didn't want to open up the leg. So then he got the idea to use the water that was pumped into the knee to aid with the vision of the scope to flush out the blade. Well we never saw it come out and with all of the water he was pumping into the patient's leg that was also flowing back out onto the floor of the OR, the room started to flood. He then decided to get an x-ray of the knee and find the blade that way. It didn't show up on the x-ray. So, he decided that it must have been flushed out and was floating on the floor of the OR. The OR Nurse was ordered to get down on her hands and knees and search for it. Before this ordeal was over, three additional OR nurses were in that room crawling around the floor looking for the blade including the Head OR Nurse a full bird Colonel in the United States Army. After an hour of searching for it and me & the surgeon standing around scrubbed in, they finally found it. The Staff Sergeant found his transfer papers the next morning and was gone. I found myself the preferred OR Tech for the surgeon and for the remainder of my time at Fort Knox I was assigned as his OR tech every time he operated because I guess we bonded during the great OR flood.

As a result of being assigned to the top surgeon, I also got to work with his right hand man a new Army Surgeon fresh out of med school. The guy was really a very nice man and so the three of us fell into a routine of being able to work together very easily. Most of the nurses were amazed that the head surgeon would work with a lowly student OR tech like me but the regular Army OR techs were thrilled because they didn't have to be terrorized by the man. Captain Elliot was the right hand man and he was a very good ortho surgeon. He only had one flaw. Every time we worked in surgery, he managed to contaminate himself or the surgical field at least once during every surgery. I always ended up having to throw instruments off the field or I would have to re-gown or re-glove the man because he would touch something that he shouldn't. The funniest time was the very last day that I worked with him. We had worked for over two hours on the case and the Boss had done everything but the final closing of the incision. At this point Captain Elliot had managed not to contaminate anything and everything was great. The Boss decided to let Captain Elliot do the final closing and the Boss left the room. As Captain Elliot and I worked on the closing, I realized that he had finally made it through a surgery without a contamination and I pointed this out to him. He laughed and he told me "I know it is amazing." Just as he said that though, he was cutting the final suture and instead of cutting the suture, he cut the tip of his surgical glove and yet again he contaminated the field. Years later, he actually ended up being assigned to my reserve unit when we went to Desert Storm. I am proud to say that by then he was no longer contaminating surgical fields.

I have just one final note about Fort Knox. I did get to participate in something fun at Fort Knox. The active duty troops put on an annual Haunted House for all of the kids on the base. I joined in the fun for the section that was done by the Hospital personnel and it was a lot of fun. Our section won for the best part of the Haunted House. I think we won because we had lots of cool equipment at our disposal to borrow or it was the real blood and body parts that we used (just kidding). I even received an Army Certificate of Achievement for my participation.

College, Military Drills & Summer Camps

I returned home right before Christmas 1984 from AIT & OJT. I was glad my training was over and I was ready to start the next chapter in my life which was college. However, I didn't start to school the next semester in January, instead, I opted to get a job and save some money to pay for my fall 1985 tuition. Luckily, I was able to find enough part time jobs that I was able to save enough for my tuition at KSU – Stark Campus for the fall of 1985.

I then spent the next two years at the local branch of KSU and earned an Associates of Arts degree in June of 1987. I then moved onto Kent State University's main campus. The problem was I didn't have a lot of money so I was living at home during college and I commuted back and forth to Kent. I also needed to work almost a full time job while I was going to school just to be able to pay for college which led me to some creative scheduling. I scheduled my classes on Tuesdays and Thursdays. I attended school all day and then I would work Mondays, Wednesdays, Fridays, Saturdays and Sundays (unless I had my Army Reserve Drill weekend and that meant I didn't work on Saturday & Sundays at whatever part time job I was working at that time).

Some of the jobs that I held while going to college were fast food, quality control at a factory, selling beer, wine, cigarettes, snacks & pop at a drive thru beverage store, stock clerk in a shoe store, housekeeping at a department store, decorated Christmas trees at a department store, and loading dock at a department store.

College to me wasn't the great college experience most people enjoyed but rather to me it was an ends to a means. Plain and simple. I did meet a lot of great friends in my classes and I enjoyed most of my classes but it wasn't my whole life. I knew that I had to pass classes in order to get the degree in order to have my accounting career. That was it.

MILITARY DRILLS

My monthly weekend drills for the Army Reserves were at times boring and at times thrilling. The people that were a part of my life through the military were like family and they have been some of my best friends in my whole life. One of the great things about the monthly drills was the fact that I made more money on those two days sometimes then I did in a whole week of working my part time jobs.

Our drills mostly were boring classes because we were a hospital and we didn't get to actually work in a hospital on our weekend drills. However, most of the classes took place in the morning and afternoons were spent doing paperwork. Then there were times when our afternoons were pure goof off sessions because there were times when we drank our lunch at the bar across the street from the reserve center and were too drunk to do anything but goof off.

I never got to join a fraternity when I was in college because of my crazy schedule and because I didn't live on campus. However, my monthly reserve meetings were like a monthly frat party. Most months at the conclusion of our Saturday drill, me and my buddies (male & female) would change clothes at the drill center and then head out. We would go to dinner, then to a movie and then hit the bars. After the bars we would go out for breakfast and then return to the drill center for Sunday. Sometimes we would get a couple of hours of sleep but most of the times we would never make it to bed. How I ever survived those weekends I have no idea but I did and I had a lot of crazy fun.

There were a couple of crazy times though where I should have been more careful but I wasn't and luckily for me in the end I managed to survive and I learned a lesson or two along the way.

One such example was a drill weekend when we went up to Lake Erie to qualify with our M-16s. I and some friends went to the shoreline to hang out after we had checked in on Friday night. We walked out on the pier and the pier had these huge cement blocks that sat on top of the pier at regular intervals. What they were for, I have no idea but we decided to climb up on one of the big cement blocks and hang out. It was a beautiful October night and it was fun looking at the stars as we listened to the lake lapping at the shore. Someone had brought a bottle of whiskey and started passing the bottle around while we sat there and bullshitted the evening away. After we finished off the bottle we decided to go to bed. I didn't think I was drunk but obviously I was. I forgot that we were up on top of the cement block and I started to walk back to the barracks. Unfortunately, I ran out of cement block and fell down to the actual pier and landed on my elbow. However, because I was drunk, I didn't think that my arm had been hurt. So, I headed off to bed. I climbed into my sleeping bag and zipped it up and fell asleep. I slept the whole night but in the morning I found I had a little problem. I couldn't get out of my sleeping bag because my arm had locked up over my chest because my elbow was broken. I couldn't use my left arm at all. My buddies helped me out of my sleeping bag and they got me dressed and off to sick call I went. I was then transported to the nearest hospital and they x-rayed my arm. They told me that the arm was just sprained and they gave me a sling and gave me pain pills. The only good thing was that because I was on pain pills, I couldn't do anything and I couldn't fire the damn M16 which was my least favorite thing anyway.

A week after I returned home, the hospital that had x-rayed my arm called to tell me that I had actually fractured my arm and that it wasn't sprained and that I should find an orthopedic surgeon.

I learned my lesson and after that I never allowed myself to get that drunk again.

ARMY RESERVE SUMMER CAMPS

Calling my Army Reserve Unit's Annual Training a "Summer Camp" made it sound like we were going off to do something fun. However, because we were a field hospital we almost always went to some crappy old army base and stayed in the field for almost the entire two week period of time and assembled our field hospital. This also meant living in tents, showering in tents, working in tents and eating in tents.

After we would get the hospital assembled we would provide first aid to other Reserve Units that were on their annual training missions as well. In addition, every year we would have to do a mass casualty exercise and usually we would have an exercise that included us having to move the hospital in the middle of the night. Without warning we would be awakened and ordered to pack up and move. It was an adventure and usually a giant pain in the butt but we always got it done successfully without injury. During our two weeks our unit always worked very hard to accomplish our missions. I am also very proud to say that we never failed any of our missions.

At the end of the day the training was just that training but along the way I got to see some things that were sometimes bizarre, sometimes funny and at other times just strange.

We once had a commander who wouldn't allow anyone to make any noise between 1 & 2 in the afternoon everyday so that he could take his nap. Yes it was the Army and yes the man wanted everything to shut down for his nap time. Like that could ever have happened in a real war situation. All I can say is that it was unbelievable. Another "summer camp" we had a fill in commander who actually threw a temper tantrum out in the field. I mean picture a man of about 45 years of age who was a hospital executive in the real world and was a Lieutenant Colonel in the United States Army and he lost it one night just because of a group of soldiers were playing a game called "What If and I would". The game was played by having everyone write down five "What If" statements on a piece of paper and five "I would" statements on the paper. The papers were then exchanged and the first person would read the first "What If" statement and the next person would read their first "I Would" statement. For example, the first person might read "What if the First Sergeant walked naked through the hospital?" and the then the next person would read "I would rather eat dirt!" Sometimes, the two statements would totally gel and sometimes they made no sense together. Of course guys being guys some of the statements that were written were very raunchy and some were about specific people within the unit. As a result the commander got very angry when someone read "What if LT. Colonel Soso joined Major Head Nurse in the shower?" Then the next person read "I would pray that God wouldn't punish the world!" Then the next question was "What if Colonel Soso had sex in his tent?" The answer was "I would ask for my inflatable doll back!" At that point he came running into the tent screaming and hollering and ordering everyone to shut up and stop playing such a game. Well, the entire time he was yelling and screaming and spitting because of how angry he was, everyone in the tent was laughing so hard. The more he yelled the more they laughed and while they were laughing everyone else in camp was laughing to. This just made Lt. Colonel Soso angrier and angrier. So what do you think was the first thing that happened after he left, the game started over however, this time, every "What If" was about him and the "I Woulds" matched perfectly and they were far from random. Lt. Colonel Soso just stood outside the tent screaming and hollering.

Another bizarre commander that we had at one of our Summer Camps was the guy that hated the food that our cooks prepared. Every night he walked through the chow line and filled his tray with food. Then as he got to the end of the line he would toss his entire meal into the trash can. Then he would get in his jeep and go eat on the post at a "real" mess hall. His leadership skills lacked a little something-something.

My first summer camp when I really didn't know what to expect before departing for it was a really crazy experience. I couldn't believe all the soldiers who were hooking up with each other. It was the first time in my sheltered life that I had ever seen married people cheat on their spouses. That just didn't happen in my neighborhood or if it did it was done with much more discretion. Out in the field there was no discretion practiced by the cheaters.

One of the funniest parts of watching these couples hook up was the fact that the couples would be inseparable the entire two week period of time. They would hold hands kiss and grope each other in front of the entire unit and then they would do God knows what in private. This behavior would even continue on the entire bus ride back home to Canton, Ohio. I would see these couples on the bus holding hands and making out and they would not want to let go until the very last moment as they stepped off the bus and then they would get off and run over to their respective spouses and lovingly kiss their spouses like they had missed their spouse ever so much. Yet, not two minutes sooner they had been on the bus with their tongue down the other person's throat.

One of my best friends in the Army was single like me and we used to talk about all the married people hooking up left and right around us while us single people behaved ourselves and that it was just odd. We also were disgusted by the fact that these couples would have intimate relations while out in the field. We were able to shower while out there but still it wasn't as clean as showering at home if you know what I mean. She and I even created a song about these couples and it was called "Summer Camp Wives".

I have never in my life been very musical so I can't describe the tune that it was sung to but the words were something like:

> Summer Camp Wives – Summer Camp Wives
> We came out to the field to play army life
> We are dirty and sweaty but yet we still get nasty
> With our Summer Camp Wife
> Oh what a double life!
>
> Summer Camp Wives – Summer Camp Wives
> I can't go two weeks without that loving feeling
> I just hope that when I get home that I won't need that
> Special penicillin healing.
>
> Summer Camp Wives Summer Camp Wives
> In my wallet are pictures of my kids right next to my condoms
> Which I must wear because I don't want a new kid calling my
> Summer Camp wife – Mommy!
>
> Summer Camp Wives! Summer Camp Wivvvves!

I think you get the message! It was bad. It was even worse on the rare occasions when we were sent to spend our two weeks working in a real hospital instead of being out in the field. Then it was a constant party after duty fueled by alcohol and more alcohol. I remember one such summer camp where a married man had driven his truck (which had a truck cap on the back of it) to our summer camp (if you asked permission at times we were allowed to drive a personal auto which then was available to be used on post for the duration, so of course everyone wanted to drive) and he came up to his Summer Camp wife (who herself was married to another man) and said to her in front of probably 20 other members of the unit and I quote "so are we going to fuck in the back of my truck or not?" Everyone in the group just went silent and we expected this woman to slap him or get angry but instead her answer was "ok" and off they went to the back of his truck which was parked maybe fifty feet from where we were all standing. Now at the time we were at Fort Bliss in El Paso Texas in July. To say that it was hot was and is an understatement but these married individuals (not to each other) climbed into the back of the truck and did it. Repeat the song from above!

However, not all of our summer camp adventures were sex related. That same summer camp while we were in El Paso, we took a unit sight seeing trip on the middle weekend to Juarez, Mexico. I was on the smaller of the two buses and our little group had a great trip. It was somewhat adventurous when at one point a Captain and I exited a shopping center from the wrong exit and found ourselves on the backside of the shopping center walking down an alley while being followed by some Mexicans who I think wanted to mug us. Thank God we had both passed our PT Test that year because we actually ended up sprinting to the end of the alley and doing a full out run to jump on the bus just before anything happened. Later that day, that same Captain and I were approached by a man on the street that wanted to take us to a private entertainment venue. He assured us that we would enjoy his daughter's donkey act (I won't go into details as to what the donkey act was but let me just say it wasn't G rated). In fact he had pictures to show us – needless to say we walked away from him very quickly.

For the most part though, my Summer Camp experiences were a lot of great memories of traveling to different places and working with people who were as close to me as my own family over the years. I was always proud to serve with my reserve unit. We were definitely one of the best field hospitals the United States Army ever had.

Chapter Five – War

CALLED TO THE DESERT
TO STAND FOR THE FREEDOM
LEGIONS WENT TO STAND ACROSS THE LINE

TWO MEN FACED OFF AGAINST EACH OTHER
SAID ONE TO THE OTHER "BRING YOURS TO DIE AGAINST
NATIONS THAT WILL UNITE AGAINST YOU OUR COMMON ENEMY"
THE OTHER STOOD TALL AND PROUD . . . KNOWING HIS WERE
SUPERIOR & HIS CAUSE JUST!

THE WORLD ALLIGNED TOGETHER AGAINST THE ONE.
TALK BY POLITICIANS THE WORLD OVER SOLVED IT NOT
SO, SHOULDER TO SHOULDER WE STOOD - MOTHERS & SONS,
FATHERS & DAUGHTERS . . TOGETHER WE SAID. .
"LET FREEDOM RING"

SO THROUGH THE ROAR OF THE MIGHTY CAME DOWN THE EVIL
IN THE END TOO MANY PAID THE PRICE BUT FREEDOM STANDS!

STANDING IN THE SILENCE LEFT BEHIND - IT IS EASY TO HEAR
AN ALL TO FAMILIAR PRAYER - - -

LET US NOT FORGET THOSE SOLDIERS
WHO PAID THE ULTIMATE PRICE - - -
LET IT BE THE FINAL PAYMENT ON PEACE
HEARD ROUND THE WORLD.

Written by Jay B. Barton
Jan 15, 1991

(Too bad this thought went unheeded and the US has been involved in numerous conflicts since 1991.)

What follows is a time line of my experiences during Operation Desert Shield and Operation Desert Storm based on a diary that I kept during the time I spent in Saudi Arabia.

AUGUST 2, 1990 - Iraq's army overruns Kuwait before dawn.

AUGUST 7, 1990 - President Bush orders deployment of U.S. Troops.

AUGUST 22, 1990 - President Bush signs an order calling up reservists to bolster the U.S. Military buildup.

AUGUST 28, 1990 - Iraq tightens its hold on Kuwait by declaring it a 19th Province.

NOVEMBER 7, 8, 9, 1990 - I took the CPA exam - spent the three days in Akron when members of my reserve unit had been instructed not to be out of town - I took my professional exam knowing that I might be in a war zone when the grades came back – I didn't think I would do to great. Boy was I right - FAILURE!!!!!!!!!!!! At least it made for a good excuse & everybody assumed that I didn't pass because my mind was on the possibility of going to war & not because I was stupid.

NOVEMBER 14, 1990 - President Bush tells Congress he is extending for an additional 90 days the 90 day call up for reservists already serving in the gulf region. They were now committed for 180 days in other words six months.

November 17, 1990 - This was one of those days in my life that I knew that I would never forget. Over the years, certain sounds and smells are still capable of bringing back the memory as though it was happening again.

November 16th was my oldest sister's birthday and as usual the entire family had been at my parent's house for a very loud and crazy birthday dinner. As usual, it was a free-for-all with everyone speaking at one time. In my family, we have always carried on multiple conversations and we always know exactly what is going on in each and every conversation and that night was no exception to the rule. It was one of those nights that were typical of my family and it was reassuring and it just made me know that I was at home.

After everyone had left or had gone to bed, I remember that I stayed up late reading a book and I remember thinking suddenly how quiet it had become. It was a quiet that made it almost feel like I was no longer in my home. Somehow, I knew that in the morning that "the call" was going to come.

I couldn't believe it that when I awoke the next morning, the house remained remarkably silent. As I awoke, all I could think was that it was strange that there wasn't anyone up and moving around the house and then it happened. "RINNNNG" "RINNNNG" the phone was ringing and it shattered the rare quiet that had fallen over the house. I froze in my bed, knowing that this was the call - the alert call – my reserve unit from Canton, Ohio was going to the Desert. I heard my mother get out of bed and walk to the kitchen with the normal clip clop of her slippers.

She picked up the phone - "HELLO, Just a moment" - then she was walking back the hall, she stopped at my door, she knocked, "Jay - the phone is for you". I asked "who is it" - the reply was "SOME MAN" & I knew that I was right it was THE CALL.

After hearing the news, I stood in the kitchen in disbelief. I always knew there was a possibility that we would be activated but I had hoped that just maybe my reserve unit would beat the odds & never get the call. So much for hope! I had work to do, so I went about the task of calling the other soldiers on my call list to notify them. As I awoke each of them, I knew exactly what each of them were thinking - what would happen to us, what would happen to our families, & when would we be back but I had to wake them and tell them to get ready to go.

After making the calls to my fellow unit members, I began calling family & friends & my employers to tell them.

As I made my calls, words of encouragement were offered by family, friends and my employers. Not surprisingly, my own father said not one word to me that day. He never offered me any support or advice. By this stage of my life, I should have been prepared for this but when I needed a father yet again, he failed me. (See deaths to know that he didn't speak because he just couldn't express himself).

November 18 -30, 1990 - The next two weeks were just a giant blur. I needed to pack my Army gear, I needed to prepare my mother to become my bookkeeper and secretary and I needed to prepare myself. It was the Saturday before Thanksgiving and suddenly it dawned on me – this would be my first Thanksgiving ever to be away from my family. It seemed impossible! Then I started to think about my 25th birthday and Christmas. Well, my mother took care of Thanksgiving by deciding that we would move it up from Thursday to Sunday. So, instead of preparing for it over 5 days, she kicked it into high gear and within 24 hours she had Turkey Day prepared for Sunday. My immediate family and N'Edna joined us for an excellent meal – sort of the Last Meal for the Condemned man. My mother even celebrated my 25th birthday complete with a cake, presents, cards and silly birthday hats.

After we spent a couple of days mobilizing at our reserve center in Canton, Ohio, the unit departed for Ft. Ben Harrison to finish mobilizing. While at Ft. Ben, we were given basic information about Saudi Arabia, we were given shots, we were given new equipment, we wrote our wills and powers of attorneys, etc. We prepared to go to war. Well some of us prepared to go to war while some of the members just did everything possible to get out of it. I was actually amazed and disappointed in a lot of the people. They had been more than willing to accept their paychecks for years and years but suddenly their country was asking them to do what they had been trained and paid for and all they wanted to do was chicken out.

As we departed Ohio, we were told that we were going to be living in tents when we arrived at Ft. Ben Harrison in Indiana. Thank goodness that we didn't have to live in tents because it would have been very cold so for the most part we were grateful for the living quarters that we were assigned to even if we were really "crowded" in the rooms. Instead of sleeping three people as the rooms were designed, we had six people in each room.

On December 9, 1990- I celebrated my 25th birthday at Ft. Ben Harrison. It was the first birthday that I ever celebrated away from my family. The thought of which depressed me and when I awoke that morning, I expected the day to be a not so good day. However, it actually ended up being a pretty damn funny birthday even if it was extremely strange.

That night the unit had a Spaghetti dinner to raise money for the unit fund. Dinner started at 6:00pm and by that time we were very drunk. We had been released from duty at about 1:00pm & we had begun drinking at around 1:30pm and we continued drinking straight through dinner. The first funny but strange event happened as we were finishing dinner and we were drunker than a skunk as some would say, Santa Claus made an appearance at our party. The only problem was the fact that Santa was as drunk as we were and for some reason he showed up wearing a gas mask, his Santa hat, his red pants and no shirt. Topless Santa wasn't your typical jelly belly Santa but rather he was a young buff soldier. Santa jumped up on one of the tables and began dancing up and down the tables knocking over drinks and just making a holiday disaster of himself. The next thing I remember was the fact that three young ladies jumped up on the table and they were dancing with him and then Santa dropped his pants to expose his special Christmas package.

By this time things were getting out of control and then someone started throwing food at Santa and his HO HO HO dancing partners. At that point, I and my friends decided to leave just as a brawl broke out among some people from another unit that had come to our party. As we were walking back to our barracks we saw the MPs responding to the Naked Santa Dance and Brawl Party.

As we continued on our walk to our barracks, we had to pass through the parking lot of the PX. All of the shopping carts were outside, so someone (me) decided we should have a shopping cart race. So we paired up and there were probably 50 people in that parking lot pushing carts with another 50 people in the carts. Carts were crashing into each other & tipping over & people were screaming & laughing. Then the MPs (military police) showed up and all of the race participants took off running with the MPs chasing us. We had abandoned the shopping carts upside down, right side up, in the lot, in the yard, and even the street. It looked like a tornado had blown through that parking lot throwing those carts around. It was a pretty funny sight made all the more funny because of the drunken state that we were in.

The next morning, the commander of Ft. Ben was extremely angry. Our unit was ordered to a formation and we were yelled at for about an hour. We were told that our behavior was not acceptable and that the Commander of Ft. Ben (a three star general) wanted the person or persons responsible or else. Well, I didn't know what the "or else" was going to be but for some reason, I decided that I needed to step forward and admit that it had been my idea. I was ordered to report to General Wellington's office immediately.

I went to his office, knocked on his door and stepped inside. I saluted and said "Staff Sergeant Barton reporting as ordered sir." The General looked up at me and as he prepared to yell at me about the shopping carts, he asked me "do I know you?" My answer was "yes sir" because I had been getting up early every morning and going to the gym to swim. The only other person in the pool every morning that early had been the General. We had struck up a conversation as we had been swimming but we had never really introduced ourselves to each other as far as our ranks and names. I had no idea prior to that meeting that he was actually a General let alone the Commander of Ft. Ben Harrison. He had told me that he had grown up in a small town close to my hometown and we had actually talked a lot about Ohio during the weeks leading up to my birthday.

He looked at me for several minutes before he finally asked "why" and I explained that it had been my 25th birthday and that I knew things had gotten carried away but it was only a momentary lack of judgment partially influenced by large amounts of alcohol on my part. He laughed and told me that he understood that but that he needed to yell at me. So he told me to sit down and he started yelling like a mad man so all of the people out in the hall could hear him yelling at me. Then after he had yelled for several minutes we just sat there and talked. He then called my Company Commander a nerdy Major (who was worthless as a commander) into his office.

As the Major walked into the room, he immediately started kissing the General's ass and said "sir Staff Sergeant Barton will be severely punished back at our unit. I am planning on demoting him to an E-4." The General looked at the Major and told him to shut up. The General informed the Major that he had punished me by assigning me extra duties in the General's office (The extra duty ended up being that I just showed up each day at around 2 in the afternoon for two weeks and answered the phones for the General's secretary so she could go do the General's Christmas shopping each afternoon) and that the Major was to do nothing to me. The General then went on to say to the Major that he understood it was just our unit blowing off steam and that while it was not to be repeated the issue was resolved.

As we walked back to the barracks, the Major told me that he didn't give a damn what that General had to say and he was going to punish me and that I was screwed. The next morning as I was swimming the General came in and asked how things were and I told him what the Major had said on the way back to the barracks. That afternoon the Major became a Captain and he was relieved of his duties with our unit. We then received a new commander who turned out to be even worse for our trip to the Desert. She was totally without a clue on how to treat enlisted people. I think she thought we were her own personal slaves plus it didn't help that she was a former Marine Drill Sergeant who had gone to college and became an officer in the Army through ROTC and she had absolutely no medical background. In real life she was a prison warden.

December 10 – 31, 1990 -As was typical of my unit during the activation period, nobody ever seemed to know what was going on. During the month of December we were repeatedly told that there was no way that we were going to be allowed LEAVE TIME to go home for Christmas 1990. Yet, at the very last minute they allowed us to go home. However, the unit said that there was no way to get everyone home and that if we wanted to go home, we needed to make our own arrangements. That is when my best friend Staff Sergeant Burkes and I took matters into own hands and we found a charter bus company willing to transport everyone home at the last moment and at a very cheap price (we played up the patriotic angle and they were thrilled to Support The Troops). Unfortunately, due to the timing, we didn't arrive home until about 7:00pm on Christmas Eve. & we had to depart Canton, Ohio about 9:00pm on Christmas day to return on time to Ft. Ben Harrison. It was definitely a whirlwind Xmas but at least it was at home. On Christmas Eve, I attended the Midnight Service at my church and surprised absolutely everyone. It was nice going home but once again we had to say goodbye & leave all over. Damned if you do & damned if you don't. When I originally left, only my mother was up & only my mother said goodbye to me as I left the house for what might ultimately be the last time. The second time to leave I had to say goodbye to my entire family and it wasn't any easier.

January 1, 1991 - Happy New Year!

I spent the first day of the New Year packing since we were to leave on the 2nd of January for Saudi Arabia and then I went to the gym to swim and basically there was nobody there working out because, they all had hangovers. The night before on New Years Eve, every member of my reserve unit had partied very hard. The things that I saw that night were beyond belief but I think it was so wild because we didn't know what we would be doing or where we would be doing it in the New Year.

January 2 – 10, 1991 - We left Ft. Ben Harrison at approximately 2:30pm on January 2nd, 1991. We went by bus to Wright-Pat in Dayton, Ohio - one bus broke down and so they were about 1 hour behind the rest of us arriving in Dayton. We got to Dayton about 4-4:30pm but by the time we unloaded our equipment and moved into the holding area it was 5:00pm. We were taken to eat (another last meal of the condemned???) and allowed to watch TV or play cards, or sleep, or whatever until 1:00am, Monday when we were supposed to leave. However at 1:00am they said we weren't leaving until 4:00am. We actually never left until after 5:00am. You had to be there to truly appreciate the total lack of organization that existed.

We flew on a chartered TWA 747. We went north and flew over Canada - everything was frozen and there was a lot of snow then east and over England and into Brussels, Belgium for a stopover - refueling & changing of crews only - none of us were allowed off! (On our flight across the Atlantic, we did get a meal and a movie) We landed in Brussels at approx. 6:00pm their time. After that stop, we were off again - we flew over Paris, France - could see the Eiffel Tower. Then we flew over Greece, Cairo, Egypt and into King Faad(??) Airport, Saudi Arabia.

It was the strangest landing - I was looking out the window – I saw absolutely no lights. It looked like we were going down into a black hole. The lights weren't turned on until just seconds before we landed. They turned on the runway lights just in time for us to land and then they went right back off. The weather was pretty nice only 50degrees. We landed about 3:00am Saudi time. After we got off the plane we stood around on the runway for about an hour then we walked about half a mile and waited a couple more hours to catch a bus ride to our new living area.

It was quite a trip. The driver was a native and the bus looked about 20 years old and it looked as though it had never been cleaned. The driver drove like a maniac and it was quite odd to be in a strange land with a driver who didn't speak English & none of us spoke his language and we had no idea where we were going and our only hope was that he did. When we arrived at the compound where we were to stay, our advance party had acquired us the luxurious accommodations of a parking garage. Yes a parking garage. I just kept thinking "Look where the Army has taken me by teaching me to "BE ALL THAT I CAN BE! It has taken me to a foreign country to live in a parking garage in a war zone!"

Eventually we moved and we were living in a strange place - a whole apartment complex with 50 - 100 buildings that the Saudis had built in about 1981 for the Nomads who then didn't want to live in the apartments and so the buildings had been empty for 10years so lots of dust inside but really nice. Each apartment had 3 bathrooms, a front & back porch, 3 bedrooms, kitchen, living room, dining room, and den. When we were inside our apartments except for the lack of furniture, you would have thought you were back home in the United States. However, when you looked outside you knew where you were because of the barbed wire and sand bags and other barriers that were surrounding the complex and all of the weapons. There were over 18,000 troops there and that number was to grow to over 30,000 troops before we left the compound. They used the parking garages as PXs and mess halls.

One night we had some excitement just before 8:00pm when some shots were fired and the entire compound went insane. All the lights went out and people were running all over the place in a panic. They believed that we were under attack. In the end, it was one of the guards accidentally discharging his weapon that set the place off into chaos. The insane panic was repeated over and over each time something happened that was out of the ordinary. I was more worried about someone killing me from within the compound just because he saw his own shadow than I was that an Iraqi would get me.

January 11, 1991 – While at the compound, we were under Threat condition Charlie the entire time which meant that we were required to wear all of our equipment at all times. However, I don't know what good our unit would have been since we were never issued any ammo. Also, all the other units were issued Flak jackets which we were never issued.

While we were in the Khobar Tower's compound, the only news we received was what we heard on the radio and it wasn't much. Later Armed Forces Radio would begin to broadcast CNN & we were able to hear the war unfold just like the folks back home.

January 12, 1991 - Congress gives President Bush the authority to wage war in the Gulf!

January 13 – 15, 1991 – By this time of my adventure in Saudi, I didn't think anyone really knew what was going on. Nobody was sure who our higher command was. Nobody was sure when we were leaving for a permanent site or when we would get the rest of our equipment that we needed. It seemed to be a huge Charlie Foxtrot (which means cluster f#&$ (rhymes with truck). I truly believed that had my reserve unit not shown up in Saudi Arabia - nobody would have ever missed us!!!!!!!!!!

However, somebody must have known we were there because it was around this time that we were ordered to have a special formation. Then we were loaded up on buses and taken out into the desert. We had no idea where we were or why we were there. When we arrived we were ordered to remove our BDU jackets and walk into a tent in our t-shirts. Inside, we were given a vaccination and sent back onto our buses. The tent was surrounded by soldiers with M-16s and we weren't given a choice to go in or not go in. In addition, our shot records were not updated. One of the Doctors from our hospital who was an 0-6 put up a huge fuss and he finally got to look at what we were being injected with which was the ANTHRAX vaccine. This of course set everyone off because this was experimental and we wanted to know why it wasn't being documented on our shot records. The doctor who got the information out of them that it was for Anthrax ended up documenting our records for us. In the end it really didn't matter because nothing ever happened to me because of that shot.

Right after the Anthrax vaccination, they beefed up the security, but all I saw was a lot of potential problems. For instance the building I was living in was the last one on the north end of the compound. The one side of our building butted up to a parking lot and a public street. I just kept thinking that it would be very easy to drive up & park a bomb right beside the building & BOOM we would have been gone. *(Little did I know but 5 years after we left this happened to that very building! At the time there were US military members still living in the building.)*

During our stay in the Khobar compound we toured a nearby active duty field hospital to see how they had set up their hospital. It was set up very similar to how we planned on setting up ours. At that point, they had been in Saudi since the 15th of August, 1990 and they were the only hospital in that area and they had done approximately 200 surgeries – mostly minor and elective type *(little did I know at that point that this would be our future also including such bull shit operations as face lifts, nose jobs, and circumcisions – more on that later)*. They had only done one major trauma case.

On the way to tour that active duty hospital, we saw several Nomad tents & Camels alongside of the road. Some of the tents looked very permanent to me. They had fences, TV. towers etc. The funniest thing to see was that at several of the tents there were Mercedes parked out front.

We had even gotten new Mercedes Ambulances for the hospital by this time because the Germans didn't send troops to Operation Desert Storm but they did send equipment including the goofy Mercedes Ambulances. The things looked extremely top heavy and they weren't fun to drive at all.

133

Each day that we were in Khobar Towers, it seemed like we had no purpose in the war. Eventually, our advance party left for our permanent site. Why they left when they really didn't know where they were going, I didn't really know other than I think our Colonel was afraid she was going to miss the entire war. According to several of the people in our advance party, when they arrived at the area where we would be stationed, they just drove around for hours until finally they found someone who decided that a certain spot was to be where we were to set up.

However, I would have been quite happy to sit in Khobar Towers until the whole mess was solved. In fact, I told some of our O.R. people that we needed to get T-shirts that read:

OFFICIAL
OPERATION DESERT
SHIELD
BENCH WARMERS!!!!

I don't know why the Colonel was in such a hurry to get to our site since there were so many problems with us being there. First, we didn't have all of our equipment, second, we weren't told that they were ready for us, and finally, as a result of the rain, our site was flooded.

JANUARY 16th - The United States launches air attacks against positions in IRAQ & KUWAIT.

The night that the air war started was quite an interesting evening. I was supposed to have guard duty at the airport but instead I went on a sight-seeing trip with the conclusion being the outbreak of a war. I had to report to the motor pool area at 6:30pm to get a ride to the airport to report by 7:00pm for guard duty. There were supposed to be four of us on guard duty but only one other guard showed up. In addition, when I arrived in the motor pool, the driver wasn't there and by the time he arrived, there wasn't anyone to be found that actually worked in the motor pool to sign the vehicle out to him. By the time he found someone to sign out the vehicle and by the time he got the vehicle signed out, it was 7:15 and still the other two guards hadn't showed up. So, we went back & forth between our building and the motor pool – until we finally found the third guard and so we decided to leave.

Our next problem was the driver didn't know how to get us where we were going. Then of course, we couldn't find anyone to give us instructions. *__(LATER, I found out that the entire staff was at the Saudi Air Force Base eating at the Mess Hall (which was supposedly off-limits to our unit) & as was typical for the duration – they (the STAFF) didn't give a damn about anything but their own comfort)__*

I finally found the Motor Pool Sergeant who gave very lousy directions but, we decided to give it a try since there were four guards at their guard posts who needed to be relieved. So, we finally left Kobar Towers at 8:30pm which was an hour & a half late. First, we headed for the pier and after a couple of wrong turns we made it there for the first drop off. We reached the pier at 9:30pm but we only had one guard for that post so one of the guards from the previous shift had to stay and the other could go back to our building. They took several minutes to hash it out but eventually they decided who would stay & who would go. With that decision made we were on the road again right? WRONG!!!!!!!!

Now we needed FUEL and of course we didn't know where the fuel point was and even though we were in the middle of the one country in the world with the greatest known oil reserves we couldn't get fuel. Luckily, the guard from the first shift at the pier who had agreed to stay at the pier knew where we could get some fuel - so he got in the Humvee & off we went to get fuel. Then we returned to the pier and switched guards yet again. It was now 10:00pm & we were three hours late for guard duty at the airport. We then took off for the airport, (we were told there would be a lot of signs) & we followed the directions that we were given. Guess what? There were no signs & we got lost. But not only did we get lost but we were on the Main Supply Route north to the front line troops at the Kuwaiti border.

Finally as the highest ranking soldier in the vehicle I decided it was time to give up the search and head back to Khobar Towers. So we turned around but we had no idea how to get back to our compound. We started driving and we got to see several very interesting local sights. At one point we came upon a check point that was only manned by Saudis - no Americans in sight but lots of weapons. So, I made the decision we weren't stopping because God only knew if they would ever let us through the checkpoint but the driver said he didn't think that he had the nerve to just drive straight thru. So, I made him get out and let me drive. I drove very slowly up to the check point, rolled down my window and I yelled "Americans" and I went straight thru their checkpoint. At this point in time I pushed the accelerator to the floor and I took off. Nothing happened - no shots and no chase – Thank GOD!

At long last at 2:00am we made it back to our compound. As we walked up to our building the "staff" (who had been eating at the Air Force Base when they should have been at our unit to give us the proper directions) was there handing out a pill to counter effect any nerve agent weapons Iraq might use because the war was about to begin. So, now I was truly angry because of what could have happened and nobody knew where we had been or what was going on. I blew up and I really let the First Sergeant have it. The chicken shit didn't even say anything back to me because he knew that they had screwed things up with not having the right people with the directions and information that I needed to get to the correct places plus the jackass knew that he shouldn't have been at the Air base having dinner when he should have been doing the briefing for guard duty.

So after I finished yelling and stopped being insubordinate, he informed me that he had relieved the other guards and posted new guards and that it was ok. In fact, he went so far as to say that I wasn't in trouble for not showing up for my guard duty. I just stood there looking at him in utter disbelief that he would make such a statement and I went into another tirade about what he could do with his "you are not in trouble bullshit". As I stood there yelling and questioning the intelligence of the Colonel, the First Sergeant, the Command Sergeant Major and the rest of the upper echelon of our unit, the remainder of the unit stood in formation and watched my melt down. Eventually, the Colonel/Prison Warden walked up and told me that I needed to let it go that a simple mistake had been made and that I needed to get into formation. I remember my response was something like a "simple mistake my ass!" I took off my helmet and threw it on the ground and just walked away. (Due to the fact that the staff knew how wrong they had been nobody even attempted to discuss my tantrum with me and for the remainder of our time in Khobar Towers, I was not assigned any additional duties. They basically just left me alone to do my own thing.)

As I walked away from the morons, I decided to head up to my room. Just as I entered the building, I could hear the Colonel start her speech to the entire unit. The speech was something to the effect that "war is about to happen" and that at 3:00am we were to get up and put on our chemical suits. After the speech, my buddies passed the rest of the information onto me when they were finally released from formation. At 2:30am we started to hear the airplanes fly over at a constant rate. At 3:00am like good little soldiers we put on our chemical suits and we all sat in our suits waiting and waiting and waiting and nothing happened. My friends and I sat on the balcony of our apartment in our chemical suits and watched the planes fly over heading to Kuwait and Iraq. We broke open a couple of bottles of Jack Daniels and toasted the start of the war. We had been told not to bring alcohol into Saudi but I and my friends had decided that with the thousands of troops that were arriving in Saudi each day, that they couldn't search every piece of luggage and so we chanced it and brought it with us.

January 18 - 23, 1991 – Every night we were kept up with the Battle of the Scuds VS Patriots – luckily our Patriot Missiles kept winning. The downside was that we were up all night in the process. The upside meant that we did nothing during the day so I spent most days reading books, playing cards with friends, writing letters home or wandering around the compound.

January 24th, 1991 – We arrived at our final site. Surprisingly, it really wasn't too bad at the Saudi Military city where we were stationed. We were set up right next to a regular brick and mortar Saudi hospital about the size of the hospitals at home. It was partially staffed by U.S. Army people. In the complex across the street was a little restaurant that we were allowed to walk to and get food if we wanted to buy it instead of eating in the mess hall. However, the only thing that they offered was chicken and rice. So, I always went in and ordered rice and chicken which the guy at the counter always responded with "no we only have chicken and rice." When we first got there, outside of the restaurant there were thousands of pigeons. When we left for home, there were no pigeons. I think we were actually getting pigeon and rice not chicken and rice.

The reserve unit that was running the hospital across the street from us got to live in fully furnished heated and air conditioned apartments complete with refrigerators, stoves, and washers and dryers. They also had the luxury of indoor plumbing.

Meanwhile, our unit was in the ghetto. We were living in tents. We were eating in tents. We were working in tents. We were showering in tents. We were attending church in tents. It seemed to be very cold there even though we had expected it to be very hot in the desert. It probably wasn't as cold as I thought it was but when you live in a tent and have to be out in the weather working it is extremely cold. I couldn't wait for the hospital to be set up so that we would have heat while we're working. It wasn't to bad sleeping since we had extreme cold weather sleeping bags but in the morning, it was terrible getting up and trying to get moving in the cold. The worst part of our experience was the toilets. They really weren't your old fashioned outhouses or the modern day port-a-johns but rather they were these wooden things that you had to step up into and they were made of plywood. The top half of the toilets were just screens so when you were sitting to do your business you looked out and saw everyone going past and they saw you. It was great waving to your friends as they passed by just like you were at home sitting on the front porch. Plus the toilets were three seaters so you never had any privacy. Quite bizarre.

We were assigned about 15 soldiers per tent and in each tent; a Staff Sergeant had been assigned the task of being in charge of that tent and its inhabitants. Why did we need an NCOIC of each tent? Our Prison Warden of a Commander thought we were in her prison. We were required to be in bed by a certain time each night and the senior person (me in my tent) in each tent had to do a bed check and report the count to the headquarters. Can you believe it – I was in a war zone and I had to do bed checks.

Things got so bad between the inmates (rank and file soldiers) and the warden (the commander) that the inmates resorted to some pretty childish behavior. However, it did provide some laughs. We rigged up a giant sling shot and we moved it all around the camp. We would load it up with garbage and fling it at our commander's tent. Some people would even urinate into their empty water bottles and sling shot them towards her tent. Nobody ever got caught and she was constantly screaming at the NCOs to catch the enlisted swine that was doing this to her. However, nobody really gave a damn about doing a thing about it because she was so abusive to our entire unit. We were always on lockdown and not to leave the camp, yet she and her "staff" were constantly going to dinner and going shopping at the places that were off limits to those of us who were the rank and file. However, I and my friends simply didn't care and we came and went as we pleased. In fact, I think the whole unit did.

January 30, 1991 – We were still trying to get the hospital set up. The biggest problem that we were having was that we didn't have all of the pieces. However, at least while we were busy doing all of the work the days seemed to go faster!

February 3 - 21, 1991 – Sand Storms, Ready or Not Open the Doors, Panic, Alcohol, & Our First Surgery.

Our first wind & sand storm started during the first week of February. It blocked out the sun and severely limited visibility. It sort of looked like Brown Fog.

After over a month of being in country, we still didn't have the hospital complete, mail was almost non-existent and we had a multitude of other problems. We couldn't complete the hospital due to the fact that we were missing about forty percent of the equipment. In regards to the O.R. we couldn't finish setting it up because we hadn't received the connector to connect the individual O.R.s to each other and to the rest of the hospital to maintain sterility. However, we did have a carpenter who figured out a way to build a connector out of plywood. The only problem was somebody higher up decided we needed to use the plywood for signs saying "WELCOME TO THE 785th ARMY FIELD HOSPITAL, CANTON, OHIO", Department signs in the hospital and a signpost like the one that had been on MASH with mileage to the different cities. So, another day went by and the O.R. wasn't ready. I guess the higher ups wanted to decorate & welcome people to our unit – it was just too bad that the patients might have died because we wouldn't have been able to perform surgery under acceptable conditions. Our leaders even went so far as to tell our higher command that our hospital was *"open for business"* a full two weeks before we ever were ready to go. The people that were leading our unit would have lied to God if they thought they could have received a little more personal glory out of it or a medal – it was like who cares if some wounded soldier comes in here and dies at least we were able to tell command that we were ready on time.

As we waited for the ground war to start, our command kept making our unit do a series of Mass-Casualty exercises. I remember one that was to begin at 1800 hours (6:00pm) but it didn't get started until 12:30am in the morning. Then about 2:00am as the exercise was going strong, the air raid sirens went off and we had to stop and put on our protective masks. The reason why the air siren went off was because someone sat on the button by accident. The damn siren was constantly going off and very rarely did it go off because of an actual threat. They were pushing the PANIC BUTTON so much that I was afraid it was going to be the real thing and that it would be ignored by half the people.

Panic and reacting to that panic was standard operating procedure at our unit. The funniest "panic story" involved garbage.

One morning a garbage truck picked up the garbage from the hospital across the street. Then as it drove away, one of the boxes of trash fell off the back, it was run over by another vehicle and then it rolled over and into the ditch that was by our perimeter. This was all observed by the two people on guard duty at our front gate. However, later one of our "SPECIAL SECURITY" personnel discovered the box lying in the ditch and decided it was a terrorist bomb and so he called the MPs. When the MPs arrived what did they decide to do? They decided it was a threat and they decided it would be better to blow it up rather than try and examine it and disarm it. They ignored the people on guard duty at our unit who tried to explain what it was and they blew it up - throwing garbage up into the air - WHAT A MESS!!!

Another funny "panic story" was the time that our "SPECIAL SECURITY" personnel thought that a stalled car just outside of our security perimeter was a car bomb. They decided that rather than evacuate the area, they the "SPECIAL SECURITY" force would surround it with their loaded M-16s until the MPs came. Why someone would think they could protect themselves from a car bomb with a loaded M-16, I'll never know.

There wasn't any beer or alcohol allowed but people did receive shipments in the mail in some pretty ingenious ways. People had it shipped inside a variety of alternative containers all because they were sure that all the packages were being searched. I had a couple of friends who sent me alcohol by just putting the bottles into a package and mailing it. The beer companies would have made a huge profit if they had been permitted to sell it in Saudi. Some did make a profit though since the non-alcohol beer was permitted. However, some people tried to make their own wine and were able to get pretty close. They saved their fruit from the mess hall and mashed it up, added sugar and yeast (where they got the yeast from - I didn't know). It was pretty amazing that some of these people were so hard up for alcohol that they did some stupid things to get it. I saw one guy drink rubbing alcohol that he stole from the hospital which of course is like drinking poison. Then there were the people who attempted to go to the island nation of Bahrain which allowed alcohol. Their plan was to buy alcohol in Bahrain and then they would smuggle it back into Saudi. Not only were they violating US Army policy they were violating Saudi law. So what did these brilliant morons do? They went to Bahrain and bought a huge quantity of alcohol and they decided to get drunk before heading back to Saudi. So, on the way off the island of Bahrain just as they entered Saudi Arabia, they crashed their truck sending beer and booze all over the Saudi highway and when the Saudi authorities arrived at the accident scene they were angry. The Saudis wanted to execute these guys on the spot. However, the US Government got involved and saved their lives. They were then sent home to face punishment. The US Government actually took the charges very seriously and they all did time in Leavenworth and they were all dishonorably discharged. Several other people in our unit also were punished as a result because they were caught with a complete list of their "customers". I was not on that list because I had alcohol that was sent to me and because I was too discreet to abuse it.

About this time, we did get our first surgical case - a gallbladder. Everything was going fine until the generator died. Since we didn't have a backup generator the case had to be finished by flashlight.

February 22 – March 30, 1991 – During the next month, I finally began to feel as if we were in a normal routine of nice days (both in weather & at work) and quiet evenings. However, as if to tell me not to get over confident, at about 5:30pm on the 22nd of February, Saddam fired 3 Scuds at us. Not just at the United States Forces but rather at our hospital or perhaps they just veered off course towards our hospital but nonetheless they came towards our hospital. Luckily, the Patriot Missile Battery that was assigned to protect us shot the Scuds out of the air. However, the explosions (about 5 of them) as the Patriots hit the Scuds were terrible. The entire O.R. shook which was quite amazing since they were tents. I think this was the closest my unit ever was to danger and I knew in that moment that I didn't ever need to be any closer.

Luckily when the ground war started in earnest, our unit received very few casualties. We did several minor surgical procedures on casualties from the battles. The most serious casualty that we received was not a battlefield injury. It was a guy who had the pin break on a grenade that he was carrying as he was sitting in his humvee. What a mess - 27 years old - broken pelvis, most of his butt gone, colostomy, and lots of infection. As our surgeon finished working on the guy he thought that he had saved the guy's life but had little hope that guy would ever walk again. However, after we returned home, we did find out that the guy not only survived but he walked again and he was returned to active duty.

Unfortunately, because we weren't sent a lot of battlefield casualties, some of our surgeons started doing a whole lot of elective surgeries. In fact, while I was out of the OR for a couple of days, there was a facelift and a nose job done. When I returned I couldn't believe that these operations had been done. I was the NCOIC of the OR Section so I put a stop to the Cosmetic Surgery business by taking all of the instruments that were needed for Cosmetic surgery and locking them up and I wouldn't provide them to the Doctors. This of course angered the morons to no end but I stood true to my principles.

The most stupid surgery that I saw performed at our hospital was a circumcision. Yes, I said a circumcision. The surgeon convinced a soldier who was not circumcised that his urinary tract infection was the result of his foreskin. Whether that was true or not, I do not know but he told the soldier that he needed to have a circumcision in the middle of a desert at a time of war. So, the soldier was brought in and the Surgeon injected the guy's penis with a local anesthetic. As the surgeon started to cut, the man screamed that he could feel the pain of the cut so the surgeon injected more local anesthetic. The patient screamed again as the surgeon started cutting. The surgeon injected more anesthetic.

However, by this time, it was obvious that the anesthetic wasn't working and that the patient was having an allergic reaction because the patient's penis was so enlarged that it was unnaturally large and was swelling even larger. A simple circumcision quickly became a nightmare. The patient ended up in the ICU for three days. All I could think was if this guy dies in a war zone because he had a circumcision, exactly how would his hometown newspaper write the story?

Eventually, because of our lack of US patients, we were shipped Iraqi POWS! We were so lucky! We eventually ended up with about 1,500 or so of them passing through our doors. We ended up doing more surgeries on POWs than on U.S. personnel. Taking care of the Iraqis really wasn't bad since most of them were extremely grateful to be at our unit. They definitely had it a lot worse in their bunkers than the US forces had it on the front lines with the bombs dropping all around. However, we were all very glad when they were gone because of how horrible the wards smelled since the POWS were just filthy when they came in. In addition several were wounded and not treated for quite some time. So there were lots of infected wounds and the wounds stunk.

Morale was never very good for our unit because of our Prison Warden of a commander; however, I think one of the lowest moments came when the unit was notified that they could send one person out of 400 plus people on an R&R stationary cruise in Bahrain. So they put everyone's name in a hat and drew one. They thought they were giving us such a great morale booster by sending one person out of 400.

While we were in Saudi, we got the chance to experience an Islamic holy month where the people fast all day and only eat after sundown. The thing that I remember the most was that the man who called the Moslems to prayer in the tower was yelling more frequently. I think that was one of the most annoying things about

Saudi Arabia. We had to hear this guy yelling over a loudspeaker several times a day. **(I know what you are thinking "Way to practice religious tolerance Jay!" but it was truly annoying.)**

I remember that on the first day of spring in Saudi, it felt like July back home in Ohio.

One night, while I had ambulance driving detail and I had driven to the airport to MedEvac People out of Saudi back to the U.S. or Germany the unit found 2 Iraqi Hand Grenades that one of the jerks in my tent had planned on taking home with himself. Anyway they confiscated the grenades and all was well. Nobody got hurt and the contraband had been found. However, this incident made me very angry. He risked all of our lives just because he wanted to take them home. Also, it made you wonder how many other idiots in our camp had explosives they shouldn't have.

March 31, 1991 – Easter Sunday – By this time we had been getting rid of a lot of patients and hadn't been getting too many in. The unit had also started to pack which was a good sign. However, there were so many rumors and no facts. I did receive a letter on Easter Sunday that was an invitation to the White House for the Vote America Foundation. I think it would have been worth the $5,000 if I could have gotten out of Saudi to go!

Easter consisted of sleeping until nine, washing my clothes, polishing my boots, picking up my mail, eating lunch, writing letters, reading, sleeping. The highlight of Easter was the fact that dinner wasn't bad - the docs bought and cooked. We had lamb kababs, rice, salad, fresh pita bread, and apple cobler.

On Easter, they took a temperature reading in three areas. One was on a piece of wood on the ground - 129degrees, the second one was in someone's hand up in the breeze - 115 degrees and the final one was in our sleeping tents with sides rolled up & with a breeze - 105 degrees.

April 14, 1991 – The Saudis finished their holy month and they started their celebrations. They decorated things with X-mas lights. Outside of our compound, there were two tanks on display and they had blinking lights all over them. They also put lights around the water towers just like we decorate our homes and Christmas trees for Christmas.

It was during this time that we did our most serious surgical case of the war. A 19 year girl (American Soldier) came in and her arm was partially severed. We worked for 5 hours just to buy her some time so that they could send her to Germany and hopefully save her arm. Thankfully her arm was saved.

April 30, 1991- We moved across the street and started using the fixed facility. The benefits were that we could tear down our hospital and be ready to go when we got a date and we got to move into the apartments behind the hospital. These apartments were really nice. They had a kitchen, dining room, living room & 1/2 bath on the first floor. On the second floor, they had 2 full baths and 3 bedrooms. They had carpeting and they were furnished. They had air conditioning, refrigerators, stoves, telephones, and washing machines. Most of our staff didn't get to work in the hospital because we were busy packing the hospital up to ship it home. I had to do both. I worked in the Saudi hospital for a couple of surgeries and I was in charge of packing up the OR. However, I was very uncomfortable in that building once I saw the attitude of the Saudi doctors. In that hospital they were kings and they ruled with iron fists and we weren't allowed to do anything about it. The hospital imported its nurses from all over the world but especially from 3rd World countries. One day, I was returning to the OR and was passing a nurses station and apparently, one of the foreign nurses had angered a doctor because he was slapping her and screaming. I wanted to step in but we had been specifically told we couldn't so I kept on walking. Luckily, after that day, I never had to return to that hospital again.

May 1, 1991 – Finally, we were told our ship date to return home was going to be May 27th, 1991.

My unit would return home on Memorial Day weekend of 1991. My life returned to normal and it was all good. I resumed my career at the accounting office where I was employed. I went on to take the CPA exam and passed. I then started to become actively involved in my community.

My service during war time was pretty average just like the rest of my life. We did our job and while we did it well we just did our job. No heroics and nothing extraordinary, yet we had earned the right to be proud of what we did. I learned from the experience yet again that I could survive under trying circumstances and I matured and I began to grow into the man that I wanted to be – a leader.

P.S. About the War. While we succeeded in forcing Saddam out of Kuwait after he had invaded it in August of 1990, we failed to bring the dictator down completely. In fact, Saddam would remain in power until April 9, 2003 and in the years following Desert Storm he committed many more crimes. He was not toppled until after 9-1-1 occurred in the United States. Ironically the President of the United States of America at that point was George Bush – son of the President Bush who was in office in 1990.

Chapter Six – Career & Community

After returning home from Desert Storm, I picked up my life right where I had left off. I resumed my career as an accountant at a small firm in my home town. I took the CPA exam and passed and proceeded forward with my life. I purchased my first home and I became involved with my community. I also ran for my first political office.

As far as my career was concerned it was an average career as a Certified Public Accountant specializing in income tax at a small local firm. I wasn't the greatest CPA but I was a good CPA. I dreaded each tax season, the long hours and tons of work but I also enjoyed developing great relationships with my clients. Plus over the years, I heard a lot of amazing things from taxpayers as they came and went through my office. I was told things by clients that they would have never told another living person but I always figured that they were willing to open up to me because they trusted me. In American society we never talk about what our total income and net worth is when we are at parties. We want people to know we are successful but not how successful we are in dollars and cents. However, when you go to CPA to have your tax return prepared or to seek financial advice you are letting all the details out. Sometimes I was shocked and sometimes I just wanted to say that is way too much information. I have never divulged those secrets and I never shall but I have surely laughed about a lot of them over the years.

One of the great things about working at a small firm, I wasn't pigeon holed into just one area of taxation. I worked on corporate returns, partnership returns, individual returns, non-profit returns, estates, and trusts.

While my career choice was to be a CPA, it was never my true calling. My true calling was volunteering and working on community projects within my home town. When I was volunteering and working on projects, I was truly my happiest. Over the course of several years, I was involved with the following:

I was involved with my church as a Deacon & an Elder. I served as treasurer, vice president and president of the Consistory and chairman of various committees. I taught Sunday school and I even preached a sermon once. (For those of you who know me – stop laughing – because yes I did preach a sermon!)

I was involved with the local Rotary Club and I served that organization as Treasurer, Secretary, Vice President and President. I was also once named Rotary Citizen of the Year much to my total surprise.

I was involved with the local Chamber of Commerce. I served as a board member, treasurer, president and chairman of the board. In fact while serving as the President of the local Chamber of Commerce, I came up with this wonderful idea to have a fundraising event that we called the Scavenger Hunt. This event really wasn't a scavenger hunt in the traditional sense. The concept was area business owners formed a team and paid a fee to participate in an evening of driving around the community from business to business in order to perform various "tasks" at each station. However, in order to get from business to business the teams had to figure out the cryptic clues that they were handed. At the completion of the race around town, the teams returned to a party of food, music and drinks. This annual event became quite the spectacle when various upstanding citizens would let their hair down and perform some pretty bizarre stunts. Examples were going to a local bar and singing whatever song the patrons requested until the patrons were satisfied with the performance, riding a child's tricycle up a hill, and many more bizarre stunts. Each year's event was centered on a theme and teams were encouraged to dress in costume. During one of the Scavenger Hunts, I certainly had one of my least Presidential moments of my life. During the planning of the event we decided the teams should hunt for a gorilla and that the team that could capture the gorilla would get bonus points. Guess who decided to dress up in the gorilla costume? That's right me! I thought that I would just wander around and that they would just coax me into their car and I would get to ride along with the team. HA! That didn't happen. When the first team saw me, one of the team members decided that the best way to catch me was to tackle me and I mean a full contact football tackle. Then while I was still dazed, I was drugged into their team vehicle and to ensure that I didn't try to escape the Tackler took off his belt and strapped it around my leg and his leg thereby strapping me to him. The team then proceeded to make a series of jokes about what they would do to keep the monkey for the entire evening and the guy I was strapped to even made some reference to spanking the monkey. Yes I was concerned for how the night would turn out.

Eventually, we ended up at one of the stations that was a bar that was owned by the mother of a friend of mine. The teams had to perform a stunt here that the guy I was strapped too couldn't perform if I was strapped to him so, I was let loose but told that if I tried to escape, he would tackle me again and then he would do more than Spank the Monkey. Well, I had seen the movie Deliverance, and since that one special scene of that movie is the image that flashed through my mind, I had no plans to go anywhere. However, I changed my mind and I took a chance to escape when the team got involved in the challenge. I ran into the bar and begged Maggie (the bar's owner) to hide me. She took pity on the big dumb gorilla and threw me into the beer cooler. As I lay on the floor of the cooler, I just couldn't stop thinking about just what had I been thinking when I decided to put on a Gorilla costume that night. Not only was it hot and humid (after all, it was August in Ohio) but now I had been captured by a group of crazy people. In the end another team found me and they were much nicer and the night ended with a lot of money being raised for the Chamber of Commerce.

I was involved with the local Scholarship Foundation as a trustee and the secretary and treasurer. This was and remains to this day a great organization. It started in 1961 with a twenty five dollar donation and has grown to over ten million dollars currently. It has provided over four million dollars in scholarships to date.

I was involved with and was one of the founders of our local Community Foundation, an organization dedicated to strengthening the community through short term projects and long term endowments. I had the privilege of serving as the first treasurer and the first president of this wonderful organization. Today that organization has over one hundred million dollars in assets.

I also was honored to serve on the Board of Directors of the local Public Library for several years. I also was honored to serve for a number of years as President of that board. My mother would have been so happy since she loved taking me and my siblings to the library.

I also had the privilege over the years to serve on many other boards and I also was very happy to provide my professional services to many non profit organizations by preparing their tax returns over the years on a pro bono basis.

The greatest compliment that I ever received for my efforts in volunteering was when an elderly woman called me to inform me that when she was growing up in Canton, Ohio, my maternal grandmother had been her Girl Scout leader and that Grandma Leeper had been one of the biggest influences on this woman because my grandmother was a caring and giving woman who also volunteered countless hours for several worthy causes. This woman told me that over the years she had often seen my picture in the paper volunteering and every time she saw my picture she always thought of my Grandmother Leeper and her volunteerism. I never met my Grandmother Leeper because she died five years before my birth, so this was nice to know that I was carrying on a family tradition and that she would have approved.

After several years of becoming involved in my hometown, I decided that I had something more to give to my community and I decided to run for City Council. I talked to everyone that I knew and I went door to door to campaign and I tried my very best. I was campaigning against a long time incumbent and I wasn't sure of my chances. On the night of the election, as the results were announced, I lost by ONE vote. Truly amazing. Yet even more amazing was the number of people who approached me at work, at church and around town to tell me that "oops I meant to go vote for you but I forgot to vote!" If all of the people who said that to me had actually voted for me, I would have won by a landside.

My job, my community activities and even my failed attempt at politics were just more experiences that helped shape me into the man that I became and have been.

Chapter Seven – The Deaths

The end of my twenties and the start of my thirties really sucked! It was a span of a year and half when my parents both passed away. As I stated in the chapter "Ancestors", I always thought of my parents as opposites in a lot of ways and even in their deaths they were very much opposite of each other. This is the story of the deaths.

Mother

Unlike my father, up until the month before her death, my mother had always been healthy. She didn't regularly see a doctor and she wasn't on any prescription medicines. In fact up until she died the strongest medicine I had ever seen her take was a single baby aspirin at any given time.

On September 8th, 1994, my mother woke up in the morning and followed her normal routine. She and one of my sisters who still lived at home were both employed at Canton City Schools and they commuted to work together. My mother spent the day working and according to her co-workers she appeared perfectly normal the entire day. However, by the time my sister had driven her home, something was definitely wrong because when they pulled into the driveway at home she couldn't remember how to get out of the car.

My father, my sister and my mother kind of laughed it off and they went into the house. My father who was retired by this time and who had become the chief chef of the house told my mom that dinner was ready and that everyone could sit down to eat. For whatever reason, that set my mom off.

I wasn't home because I was living in my first home by that time. In fact, I was on my way to a meeting with a client when my cell phone rang. (Note: this was 1994 and cell phones were pretty new at that time and I had just two weeks before this bought my first one. Had I not had it, the remainder of the evening's events would have been different because my family would not have been able to reach me as I drove to my client's. When I say the evening's events would have been different, they could have been better or they could have been worse.)

My sister told me that she thought that I should stop by the house, because my mother was acting kind of strange. I explained that I was on my way to a meeting with a client and that I would stop by on the way home unless it was an emergency. As I was saying "unless it is an emergency", I heard my mother in the background tell my dad to "shut the hell up about his dinner because she wasn't going to eat the shit that he had made". For the first 28 years of my life, I had never heard my mother swear and so I knew that it was a real EMERGENCY! I immediately called my client and told them that I had an emergency and I detoured myself to my parent's home.

When I arrived at the house, my mother was in a very agitated state and she was screaming at everyone. My mother had in her hands two advertisements from the newspaper. One was an ad from Montgomery Wards (an old department store) and the other ad was from a local nursery advertising its tulip bulbs for fall planting. Her problem with the ads was the fact that she couldn't understand why the tulip bulbs were 10 for $ 5 and the washing machines at Montgomery Wards were on sale for $ 250. She kept saying that they should be the same price.

I talked her into putting down the ads and I got her to sit down in her favorite chair in the living room. As I started to get her calmed down, my father walked into the living room and that only agitated her more. I asked my family to stay in the kitchen so I could calm her down. Finally, I managed to calm her and I started talking to her. I was asking questions such as "who am I?" "What is your phone number?" "What year is it?" etc. In spite of her sudden preference for cussing and swearing and her price comparison confusion on comparing tulips to washing machines, she knew the answers to all of my questions.

My sister eventually ventured into the living room with a plate of food. I talked my mom into eating dinner and I even asked if my father could sit in the living room with her. She agreed and I left my mother, my father and my siblings in the living room. My mom even asked my dad to turn on the TV so they could watch one of their favorite TV programs.

I left the living room to go call my mother's physician and of course I reached his service. While I waited the thirty minutes that it took Dr. Davidson to return my call, I had to deal with another "delightful incident" from my mother. While I was on the phone she had acted like she was eating her dinner. In reality all she had been doing was stuffing food into her mouth. My sister was trying to get her to spit it out since she wasn't actually eating it. My father was yelling at her because he had lost his patience and when I got in the living room, there my sweet mother sat in her chair with fat cheeks full of food giving my father the bird. Once again I calmed her down, got her to spit out her food and I got her to stop flipping off my father.

Finally, Dr. Davidson returned my call. After I explained what was going on with my mother, he told me that if we took her to the emergency room, more than likely that the hospital would admit her for a psychiatric evaluation. Instead he suggested that I just bring her to his office the following morning. I agreed because I obviously didn't want my mother to face a psych evaluation.

I told my family what was going to happen. My father looked at me and said "you are going to spend the night here right since she only seems to listen to you!" I hadn't thought about that but decided it would be for the best. At that point my other sister who didn't live at home, arrived to check on what was going on and she had brought my mother a milkshake because she knew that my mom loved them. I left to drive home and get a change of clothes. I forgot to turn on my cell phone (a trait that would follow for many years after that but that is a whole other story). As I walked in the front door of my house my phone was ringing and as I answered it, it was my sister screaming that I needed to get back to my parents home and I needed to do it now.

I raced back out the door and sped to my parent's house that was about two miles from my home. I was going well over the speed limit because of the fear that had been in my sister's voice. It seems that after I left my mother decided to get a spoon to eat her milkshake rather than sipping on it through a straw. However, she really wasn't planning on eating it with the spoon. Instead she had decided to use the spoon to flip milkshake at everyone that was in the room. Milkshake was all over the room. My mother was screaming, cussing and throwing things at whoever moved in the room. I managed to get her back into her chair and calmed down.

I decided to call Dr. Davidson again and as I waited for the call back, my mother suddenly became unresponsive and slumped down in her chair. I immediately thought she had a stroke. Right then the doctor called back and I told him what was going on and that we were headed for the ER. We called 911 and the ambulance came and we went to the hospital.

It was as if my mother's entire body was shutting down. She was almost in a coma. As we waited in the ER I just kept thinking we would never take her out of the hospital. After many tests and no conclusive findings, the ER doctor admitted my mom at about 2:00am. As my family and I returned home, I was sure she wouldn't make it through the night.

The next morning when we returned to the hospital my mother was awake and almost back to normal as far as being able to talk and control her body. However, mentally, she was acting like she was a child. Doctor after doctor examined her and there wasn't a diagnosis. Finally after all the many tests and exams, eventually, they found out what was going on. The doctor called us out into the hallway and in a matter of fact no nonsense manner, he told us:

She had an inoperable brain tumor.

She was terminal.

She would probably only have three to six months.

We brought my mother home on the 16th of September. Little did we know the tumor would run its course a lot faster than the doctors anticipated and she would pass away on October 16th, 1994.

However, that month was in some ways the longest month of my life. My siblings and I took care of our mother around the clock. We became the nurse to her that she had been to us during the years we were growing up. There were moments that were the saddest moments of my life and there were moments when my mother made me laugh so much that I couldn't believe that I was laughing while she was dying.

Because of the tumor, my mother wasn't walking to steady so she had to use a walker to get around. However, one day she decided when it was just her and my father at home that she needed to go down to the basement to check on her flowers that were growing in the basement. In reality there were no flowers growing in the basement. They were a figment of her altered reality. My mother had walked down the stairs with her walker in her hands. When I arrived at the house I couldn't find her and when I asked my father where she was he had no clue. I heard something in the basement and when I went to investigate I found her in the basement looking at flowers that weren't there.

When I tried to explain to her that she shouldn't have gone down to the basement because of her difficulties with walking and furthermore that she could have fallen down the stairs while trying to carry her walker with her and she just laughed at me. She looked at me with a straight face and said "it's ok - if I would have started to fall, I would have just changed myself into a beach ball and then I could have bounced down the stairs and I would not have gotten hurt!" Her statement was very funny and I wanted to laugh but I couldn't.

Another time, we had watched an episode of the Brady Bunch where Greg and Bobby get locked in the meat freezer at Sam's butcher shop. Later that day, an old friend of my mother's stopped by to visit with my mom. As they sat on the front porch of the house and chatted my mother related the Brady Bunch story to her friend. However, she substituted herself and her grandson for the Greg & Bobby characters. She had her friend believing that we had allowed her and Danny to go to the basement and get locked into a room. I explained to the woman that it was an episode of the Brady Bunch but I didn't think she believed me because Mom was very convincing in telling her story from her altered state of reality.

During my mother's illness and death, I truly experienced the power of God. The night that we found out that my mother had an inoperable brain tumor and was going to die, my deceased Uncle Bruce showed up at my house (in a dream) to reassure me that though my mother was going to die, I and my family would survive. I was in bed and the doorbell rang. When I went to the front door Uncle Bruce was there with a huge bunch of white roses. He handed me the roses and said "everything will be all right – don't worry." When I woke the next morning, I was no longer feeling sorry for myself but rather, I was at peace because of what I thought had been a dream. However, my whole house smelled like roses. In fact the smell of the roses never left my house until after my mother's death. I know some of you probably think that I was imagining that smell but every person that came into my house during that month smelled the roses without me saying a single word about my Uncle's visit.

The second time that I had a very spiritual experience was the day that my mother died. I woke up at about 5:00am on a Sunday morning. I wasn't able to fall back asleep and I just needed to go visit my mother. I showered and dressed and drove out to my parent's home. When I got there everyone was still in bed so I let myself in and walked back the hall to the bedroom where my mom's hospital bed was set up. As I walked back the hallway, I heard two things. I heard a tapping noise and I heard my mother talking to someone. As I entered the room my mother smiled and said "good morning Jay" which just shocked me because during the month since her diagnosis, my mother hadn't recognized anyone by name. She then told me to come on in and have a seat and visit with everyone. I asked her who else was in the room and she just looked at me and said "why all these people of course." There was only her and I in that room yet there she lay talking to all sorts of people who I knew were dead. Oh yeah the tapping thing was because she had taken her wedding ring off her ring finger and she had placed it on her thumb and she was just obliviously tapping away on the metal rail of the hospital bed.

As I sat there talking to my mother who was actually coherent, she finally asked me if she was going to die. I looked at her and I couldn't say the word, I just shook my head up in down to mean yes. She smiled and said that she knew it and that her brother Bruce had told her that she would be ok and that she had given him directions on how to get to my house so that he could tell me that it would be ok also. She asked if he had come over and brought me the white roses that she had sent. Again, I was speechless.

My mother fell back to sleep and I left the house and went to church. While I was sitting in church, I heard someone say "today is the day your mother is going to die. You need to be with her all day." I heard those words as though the person who said them was sitting right next to me. It was a man's voice yet the person sitting next to me was a woman. It was then that I knew that my conversation earlier would be my last conversation with my mother because that day would be the day that she would die. Surprisingly, I was at peace with it because of the voice.

The remainder of the day, my mother's condition worsened and that evening around 6:00pm my mother passed away surrounded by her five children and her husband. We had had time to prepare yet weren't prepared. However, we survived and we were there for each other.

Father

While my father's health had not been good for a number of years, he suddenly seemed to be holding his own. In fact, while mom had been sick, he had seemed to pick up and he had even seemed to have improved. However, within a year and a half of my mother's death, my father would also be dead.

With my mother we were given a diagnosis and we were given time to be with her and to say goodbye. With my father that was not to be the case. Instead, he suffered a massive heart attack and was gone before any of us knew that there was a problem. My younger brother and oldest sister found him on the kitchen floor.

I don't know why but while I remember my mother's illness and actual death, I really don't remember her calling hours or her funeral. In my dad's case, I remember the funeral more and I don't really recall much about the day that he died.

One of the important things that I remember about his funeral is the fact that in spite of his racial intolerance in life, his funeral was attended by several African Americans. Happily, they weren't there seeking satisfaction in seeing him dead from some wrong that he had done but rather they were there out of love and friendship. Several were people that had worked with my mother over the years and who my father had come to recognize as friends because he actually took the time to get to know them as people and not simply as the color of their skin. Some of the African Americans were there out of friendship for me and my siblings. I loved the fact that in spite of what he had said and taught us, that each of us had learned to value friendships on a personal level based on common ground and not a common skin tone.

While at the cemetery, I experienced my father's death on a whole new level that left me feeling very alone. After the ceremony at the cemetery, I was standing alone because each of my siblings had walked off with their spouses and their children. As the one sibling that was single and without children, I truly felt alone that day. As I stood there I thought to myself, I am an orphan. I know that might sound weird in so much as I was thirty years old at the time but technically since both of my parents were now gone, I was an orphan. It was like one of those scenes from a movie when a character stands in the center of the street as everyone and everything moves in slow motion around him and he observes it all while the camera pans around him. I saw each of my sisters with their husbands and children. I saw my brother with his wife and his child. I saw mourners returning to their cars. I saw the cemetery people lowering my fathers casket into the ground. All the while I couldn't move and I was just feeling so angry.

I was angry at my father and myself because I had never gotten the chance to resolve my issues with him. I spent a large part of my life not wanting to be like him and feeling as though there was no love lost between him and me. As I stood there watching everyone move away, I was finally brought back to reality when one of my father's friends handed me a letter that he told me to read later when I was alone.

It was a letter from my father and it freed me from the feelings that I was having while standing in the middle of the cemetery. For so long, I felt as if I hated my father and that he hated me. In fact, I often thought that I didn't want to be my father's son. I even used my feelings about him to distance myself from any chance of having a relationship that would have allowed me to get married and have children. Yet when I finally read that letter, I was finally able to let it all go. What he hadn't been able to say in life, he managed to say in death and he finally said what I had always wanted to hear.

Dear Son:

I am proud of you and I love you.

Your Dad

It was dated and even notarized. He had written it in 1991 while I was in Saudi Arabia for Desert Storm.

It inspired me to say a prayer to God to ask my dad to forgive me. I wondered that day if I would be lucky enough to get into heaven to tell my dad I was sorry. I wondered because after so many years of damning my father to hell, I was somewhat worried that I might be heading to hell myself because I had never bothered to utter those words to him while always holding it against him that he hadn't said them to me.

After my father's death my life continued on as it had been. I continued to work as a CPA and I continued to volunteer within my community. Prior to the Presidential thing, the most exciting and not so average thing that I ever did was to write two books that were published.

Chapter Eight – The Books that I've Written

In the years leading up to my run for President of The United States of America, I spent what little free time that I had writing two books. I really enjoyed writing each of the books. What follows is a brief recap of the books that I previously wrote. So, if you are enjoying my memoir please go online and purchase my other books. I could use some extra income from the royalties.

Dandelions for Retirement

This was my first book and I wrote it as a CPA giving retirement advice in a not so conventional manner. The book idea actually came to me one hot summer day as I mowed my lawn. As I was mowing, I noticed that my yard was just covered in dandelions while no other lawn in my neighborhood even had a single dandelion.

I began to feel ashamed that my yard was contaminated as compared to all of my neighbors. Then a couple of nights after that observation of mine, I was having a conversation on the sidewalk with several of my neighbors. You the know the type of conversation where the adults in a neighborhood gather to socialize, partake of a beer or two and then try to solve the world's problems. It was that kind of neighborhood meeting.

During that meeting my neighbors started razzing me about the dandelions that were in my front yard. I kind of sheepishly said "yeah I know and I really should do something" but before I could really commit one of the neighbors told me that it would cost around $ 2,000 per year and my yard would be as beautiful as all the rest in the neighborhood. I said that I'd look into the situation.

Well that night I got to thinking about spending $ 2,000 to kill something that was growing naturally in my yard and that wasn't really hurting anything or anyone. I also got to thinking that dandelions are edible and that a person can make wine from them. Most importantly, I was thinking about the fact that I didn't want to spend $ 2,000 per year to kill dandelions and to make my grass grow more. If the yard was going to grow more then it would just need to be mowed more which would just take more of my time and more of my money.

I got to thinking about the fact that only in America would people spend $ 2,000 a year to fertilize their lawns and kill dandelions just to make the yard grow more, just so they would have to mow more frequently and complain more about the high cost of gasoline. My neighbor who told me the $ 2,000 figure for all of the lawn treatments was actually at the time mowing his lawn every third day. I mowed once a week and sometimes I stretched that out to every 9 days.

The numbers were crazy and the whole concept made no sense to me.

I just couldn't do it. I mean those dandelions just weren't a threat to anyone. They weren't weapons of mass destruction and they didn't deserve to be terminated.

So the next time the neighbors all got together on the sidewalk the chemical treatment guy was there and he was ready to make a sale to me. He said "are you ready to get rid of those dandelions and let me fertilize that lawn to make it green and beautiful like all the other lawns?" I stopped him in his tracks by asking what chemicals were in his treatment and how safe they were. He couldn't name all of the chemicals but he was sure that they were safe. I asked if they were safe to soak into the ground where they would eventually find their way into the drinking water and I also asked if they were safe to be played on by pets and children. He stuttered and stammered and said they were relatively safe. At that point, I excused myself and went inside and got a big tall beer glass. I returned to the sidewalk and asked him if he would fill up my glass with the chemicals that he wanted to spray on my lawn. He and my neighbors all looked stunned and said "WHY?" My response was that I would place those chemicals on my lawn when and if the guy would drink a full glass of the chemicals. When he refused to drink the chemicals, I asked if he wanted to come inside where we could fill up my bathtub and he could take a bath in them. If he would do that to prove they were safe, well then he could feel free to spray away.

I had drawn a line in the sand! I wasn't going to do something just to keep up with the Jones as they say.

After that it just seemed logical to tell my clients that they too could draw the line at something and if they did draw that line at a certain expense and if they put that money away each year, they would be saving towards retirement.

The whole book became ideas on what to draw the line at and I even went so far as to say that not only was I saving money by not spraying those chemicals on my lawn, but I was also making money by harvesting the dandelion greens for salads and selling the dandelions to area people who like to make dandelion wine. In fact, every year after that I would have at least one salad from my front lawn's dandelion patch. I would go out and set up a table. Pick the dandelion greens. Wash them with the hose. Chop them and add some other ingredients and toss a salad on the front lawn and then dine on them. My neighbors thought I was crazy but hey those dandelions inspired me to write a book that produced some extra income for me and a free meal.

Single Member Christianity

My second book had nothing to do with finances or taxes or anything within the scope of my professional life. Instead it totally had to do with my spiritual life. I actually started this book before the other one but it took me quite a bit of time to finish because I wanted it to be just right. Why? Because I was challenging organized religion with it and I wanted to have everything that I wanted to say down just perfect before I submitted it to be published and before another living soul ever read the book.

In 2005, I started to lose my faith in religion as defined by man. I never lost my faith in God the father, God the son and God the Holy Spirit. However, I had had enough with man and his interpretation of what religion should be.

In 2005, I broke my leg while mowing the lawn. (Yes I know that sounds stupid but it is true). I did a pretty good job of breaking it too because I was in a cast from my toes to my hip for 16 weeks that summer. I also did not walk using that leg until 6 months after the break. Anyway, during my hospitalization, surgery and recuperation, my church severely let me down. Now I want to emphatically state that the majority of the individual members were of great service during this time but there were some doozies that really made me wonder about the church. One member actually told me that perhaps God broke my leg as a way of telling me to slow down. Excuse me but am I to believe that God is like Vinnie the Enforcer and when he isn't happy he breaks your leg like Vinnie the Enforcer would do if I owed money to a bookie? I don't think so.

In addition, to my disappointment with my own church members, I started looking for articles in newspapers and magazines that were about churches. The more that I read the more things just didn't make sense to me.

There was a minister in Rhode Island that removed a female Sunday school teacher based solely on his interpretation of the Bible that God didn't want women to speak when they were in the churches. Now the lady in question had been a Sunday school teacher for over 40 years. Yet, this bozo of a minister wanted her to step down because now all of sudden he was going to enforce the idea that God wanted women to remain silent in the church.

There were way too many articles about Mega Churches which were in fashion in 2005 where the articles talked about the thousands of people who were members of the churches. I didn't understand how you could be one of thousands and still expect to receive that special fellowship that most parishioners feel with each other. In addition, I started looking at the budgets of several churches and what was the number one largest expense on every budget? That's right salaries and in most cases the Ministers salary was the majority of the salaries item. It didn't make sense to me any more how the minister could preach about stewardship and tithing. I couldn't accept ministers saying that the church needed so much money and it was the obligation of the parishioners to supply it when in fact the majority of the money was going to end up in the minister's pocket. It was as if the ministers were working on commission. I don't think it takes an expert to know that ethically it doesn't work for someone who is going to financially benefit to be openly advising another person as to what they should do. This is especially true when the person doing the advising is saying that it is the parishioner's obligation to tithe if the person wants to make God happy.

I also developed a strong dislike for those who would use the Bible as a club to enforce their wills on another. They would take one tiny piece of the Bible and interrupt that piece as they wanted it to read so that it benefited their own purposes and not the purposes of the rest of the world.

It was then that I decided that what was most important about religion was to have a one on one relationship with God. Therefore, I wrote the book titled "Single Member Christianity" and it was meant to serve others as they thought about whether or not they had a need to be ruled by religion as interrupted by man or rather they just wanted to read their Bibles and pray to God and have that one on one relationship with God. In the book I encouraged my readers to A) continue their relationship with their church if they were happy B) investigate other possibilities if they weren't happy and C) always maintain an open conversation with GOD. Option C was and is the most important component of everything because none of us need to be told when, where and how to pray to God. None of us need to contribute financially to a church in order to speak to God and live according to how the Bible in its entirety would have us live our lives.

This book wasn't well received by the Church going public at large because I think the ministers were afraid of what my message was going to do to the bottom line. For those who read my book, it did suggest that people shouldn't give to a church's budget, just so that the majority of their money ended up in the hands of the Senior Pastor. However, I did suggest that the readers spend their alone time with God and then take the tithe they would have made to the church and donate it to an organization that they knew would use the majority of the money to assist those in need and not for overhead or that they should just give the money directly to someone in need.

I am proud to say that a lot of people enjoyed reading the book because they too had the same feelings that I did that Man's version of religion was failing us and that God's version never fails us. I also loved the idea that it was time to remove the middleman and deal with God one on one.

Chapter Nine – The Presidency

I was elected to the Presidency because a group of very wealthy individuals decided to challenge the Status Quo of the Republican Party vs. the Democratic Party in 2016. They spoke about the need and desire to put "We the People" back into government and more importantly put a President of the People back into the White House. However, their real goal was to spotlight the failures of the two parties and effect change by challenging both parties to realistically evaluate their shortcomings. The group never actually intended for their "average" candidate to succeed. Unfortunately for them, I succeeded due to some unforeseen circumstances.

This group decided to pick their candidate with a sweepstakes. Each applicant/contestant had to submit a resume and essay on what the Office of President of The United States of America should mean. They promised the winner a prize of one million dollars and that was my true motivation for entering the contest. I always enjoyed entering sweepstakes and contests and this one was promising at least one million dollars plus if the campaign was successful the winner would be awarded full time job for at least four years with a house and private jet. So, I entered the contest.

As the winner of the contest, I was obligated by a signed contract to allow the "We the People" committee to run the campaign. They ran the entire campaign and I had absolutely no say in what happened. The only real message of the campaign that the "We the People" committee tried to convey was that it was time for a change from partisan politics to a new era of government being for the people and that to accomplish this America needed a candidate that wasn't an insider and one that had not been corrupted by politics as usual.

All I had to do was get on a private plane or on a private touring bus and travel around the country and appear at their selected events. The only part of the campaign that was me was when I was interviewed by the media. During interviews I was allowed to answer the questions according to my own opinions only because the "We the People" committee managed the interviews in such a manner that they only allowed certain members of the media access to me and they always controlled which questions the media could ask of me. Accordingly, since the committee knew where I stood on the issues, they only allowed me to be asked the questions that I would answer in accordance with their opinions.

At the same time, I, as a candidate, was lucky that the "We the People" committee never put forth any substantial policies and they never made campaign promises so after I was elected; I wasn't left holding the bag on a bunch of their policies. The result was that my campaign was never taken seriously by the two major parties or by the media. It was only taken seriously by the real American people because they were tired of the status quo and the tightly managed message actually resonated with the public and I never had the opportunity to misspeak. Plus, since the major candidates didn't take me seriously, they didn't dig up dirt to throw mud on me. However, they both did a lot of digging of dirt on each other and the throwing of mud at each other. Their mudslinging and destruction of each other is what actually put me into office.

Three days before the election, both parties dumped so much mud on each other that they totally destroyed each other and neither side had the chance to spin doctor anything. The only votes that either candidate received were the votes of the truly die-hard faithful and even the die hard faithful had a difficult time voting for their candidates after what they revealed about each other. It was revealed that one candidate had embezzled from the people of his home state (over five billion dollars) when he had been the governor of his state. The other candidate was actually arrested on murder charges three days before the election. It had always been whispered that he had murdered a college roommate and the opposition actually dug up the smoking gun that proved he was guilty beyond a reasonable doubt. After my election both of these candidates were on their way to the Big House (prison) as I headed for the White House. So because of the biggest political mudslide in history and because of the fact that the "We the People" campaign had actually gone to the trouble to get me on the ballot in all 50 states and because they had micromanaged the campaign, ninety percent of the voters voted for me.

After the election results came back, both parties insisted that it was absurd that a nobody like me could be elected. They put forth proposals that the Electoral College should ignore the popular vote and that each party should be given the right to name a substitute candidate because it just wasn't fair how everything had happened. The media also jumped on the Ban Barton Bandwagon as well. Every talking head that could get on the air spoke out and condemned me and my presidency even though I hadn't served one single day. The incumbent president even suggested that he should stay in office until new candidates could be found for the Republican and Democrat parties and a new election could be held.

However, the "average" citizens of the United States of America united and said "HELL NO!" There were massive demonstrations all over the country demanding that I be allowed to take the oath and become the 45th President of The United States of America. In the end the "career" politicians feared the wrath of their constituents, the media jumped on the "average" angle and the

172

Electoral College bent to the will of the popular vote and I had become the 45th President of The United States of America.

Preparations

The very first thing to happen after it was certified that I was to be the next President was that I was sued by the "We the People" committee for breach of contract. The committee thought that they were the true winners of the presidency and that I was going to be their puppet. They wanted to call the shots and they quickly learned that I had other ideas. The short and sweet version of the story is they sued, they lost, they appealed all the way to the Supreme Court and they lost. After losing the battle for them to take control, of my presidency, they next sued me to reimburse them for the campaign costs. Again they lost because I never breached any clause of the contract that they had written and had forced me to sign when I won the contest. In the end, I was awarded attorney fees plus I received my one million dollars of contest winnings.

Of course I had no clue about preparing to be the next President. I didn't know who to hire and I didn't know who to appoint and I had no idea of the extent of the multitude of other preparations that lay ahead of me. However, I managed to think my way through the process and this is what I did. First, I talked to the outgoing President who was actually very supportive (once it was decided that he wasn't going to stay on after the post election mess about whether or not I was truly the President Elect) and he gave me several good suggestions. Second, I went to the top Republican and I went to the top Democrat and I asked each of them to make a list of who they would suggest I appoint to each and every position. This was pretty funny because both sides went to the media after I made my request to let the world know that they had been asked for assistance. Both sides were trying to suggest that I was swinging towards the right or towards the left. When it came out that both sides had been asked the media thought that they had a big story to tell and they tried to suggest that I had no clue. I simply responded by telling the truth which was that I wanted the best person for each appointment that I was about to make and I had sought out information from both sides in an effort to be bi-partisan.

After the posturing of the two sides and the media trying to exploit a non-story, I finally received the two lists. I then took the two lists home to Ohio and I gathered all the people from my home town that I respected and whose opinions I valued. This group was comprised of Republicans and Democrats but most importantly it was comprised of taxpaying citizens who were ready for any change that would benefit the country. The committee and I then reviewed the two lists. In three instances, the Republican and the Democrat had both suggested the same person for the same position. I contacted the three individuals and they were on board. My group of advisors then helped me to review the remaining list and we looked at the qualifications of the people who were recommended and then we found people that we knew who had the same qualifications and those are the people we went after to join my administration. This circle of friends that I gathered for that review process also officially became my most trusted advisors throughout my Presidency.

Inauguration

My inauguration was another huge departure from recent memory. I have never understood why millions and millions of dollars needed to be spent on one day & night of parties. Several corporations offered to sponsor the night's events but I refused each offer. My idea of the perfect inauguration was to actually have the swearing in ceremony followed by late lunch with my family and my closest friends. The guest list to the lunch was kept at 200 people. Several politicians who believed themselves to be at the top of the political food chain made no attempt to hide their displeasure in not being invited to join my lunch but I had no regrets. Some even swore up and down that I was damaging the image of the office of The President of The United States. They said it was "my obligation" to have the pomp and circumstance in order to convey the true prestige of the office. I still refused. To me it was and is a waste of taxpayer dollars or worse the brazen attempt of major corporations to curry favor with the White House. I was determined to start my Presidential career without wasting taxpayer dollars and without owing political debts.

At my swearing in ceremony, I also limited who spoke and who participated. All the people who believed themselves to be the "important" people of Washington D.C. were invited so that they could have their dog and pony show but they did it on my terms. My speech that day was extremely short because I got straight to the point and said what I meant and that was it. I didn't stand up there and make pie in the sky promises and I didn't try to be politically correct but rather I told it the way I saw it and the way that I believed it. In addition, I was not about to be like every other politician and begin campaigning for reelection on the same day that I took office and I didn't use my speech to kick off my next campaign.

THE SPEECH

My fellow Americans, today I become your 45th President. I do not become President under normal circumstances. I have never served politically on the national stage and I have not served politically on a State level in my great home state of Ohio. My only prior foray into politics was when I ran for City Council in my hometown and lost by 1 vote. After that heartbreak, I thought that I would never run again. Yet I did and here I am.

I am neither a Democrat nor a Republican.

I am however, an average American. I have experienced the ups and downs of every other average American.

I have served my country as a member of the United States Army and I am a veteran of Operation Desert Storm.

I am not famous and I do not claim to be the greatest at anything. I believe that I have been responsible for my own life and I have always made good decisions in my life. As such I can relate to the millions of other responsible Average Americans.

I am tired of the extreme right and extreme left agendas of Career Republicans and Career Democrats taking center stage at the expense of ideas and ideals that could serve the Average American so much better.

In this country it is easy for the career politicians to address the issues of the very rich because they are the ones who have the money to contribute major dollars to the political campaigns and as a result in Washington DC the voices of the very rich are heard.

It is also very easy for the politicians to reach out to the "poor" in this country and give them Earned Income Tax Credits and Welfare checks because it is easy to say "I am doing the right thing by helping those who are at a disadvantage."

The worst part of politics as usual is the fact that both traditional parties in this country overlook those of us who are neither rich nor poor but rather are the Average Americans. We are the citizens who get up each morning and go to work to earn a paycheck. We then take those paychecks and budget our money. We pay our bills, including our mortgages and health insurance without assistance from the government. We find a way to stretch our budgets to pay for gas for our cars when it increases 40 or 50 cents per gallon overnight. We don't buy homes that we cannot afford and then ask the government to bail us out when things go bad and we can't afford the monthly payments. We the "average Americans" find a way to send ourselves and our children to college. We endure each administration whether it is Republican or Democrat. It is we the "average Americans" that suffer most with each new tax but at the end of the day we stretch the budget a little further and pay our taxes and get by as Americans...

.

Today, I accept the challenge of becoming the President who wants to be the voice of the Average American while at the same time being the President of the United States without political clout and without support of a political party. Most of the political insiders and talking heads on television will tell you that my entire Presidency will be a lame duck presidency. However, I am here today to tell you that I am prepared to be a Presidential advocate for my fellow average Americans. Each decision I make will be based on what I believe is best for the majority of Americans. The big money contributors no longer have the ear of the oval office and I have no political debts to repay.

I pledge to you today that I will try my best to effect change. Each decision that I make will be made keeping in mind that it must be in the best interest of the Average American taxpayer.

Now before I go any further, I want to define what exactly I mean by an American taxpayer. An American taxpayer is any individual who actually pays out more in taxes than they receive in direct government benefits in the form of refunds, tax credits and public assistance. So you need to add up the amount of Federal Taxes that you pay into the system plus Social Security taxes paid plus State income tax plus Real Estate tax plus sales tax minus all

*refunds, credits and direct assistance you receive in order to
determine whether or not you are a taxpayer.*

*For example if you receive an Earned Income Tax refund for tax
year 2015 and it is for $ 4,500 and it is greater than all the other
taxes you paid guess what you are not a taxpayer. You are a
recipient of Federal Aid paid for with the tax dollars of the
American Taxpayers.*

*I promise that I will make my decisions based on what is best for
at least 51% of the American taxpayers. I also will only make
decisions based on what is best for the majority of United States
Citizens.*

*If you are an illegal immigrant my decisions and my policies will
not be beneficial to you and you are not going to like my decisions
and my policies. If you don't like what I have to say and how I say
it I would suggest you get out now before I have the chance to
deport you. For those illegal immigrants who haven't bothered to
learn our English language you will wish that you had.*

*Finally for those of you who are on welfare and public assistance,
I will say this, I am not opposed to assisting those of my fellow
Americans who are in need. However, Welfare is not a
constitutional right and welfare is not a way of life. I will be
proposing broad changes to America's welfare policy. My
proposed changes will be keeping in mind that I answer to those
Americans who are actually taxpayers. As a nation we will assist
those in need however it will be done with a new era of assistance
with accountability. Accountability by the government and
accountability by the recipients.*

*For those public servants who believe that decisions should be
made on a partisan basis and on partisan ideals, you now have an
Average American in the White House. If you make decisions*

based on anything other than what is best for the majority of TAXPAYING citizens, I will be there to call you out. I may not change your behavior but I will do my best to point out your lack of concern for the majority of taxpayers and hopefully at the next election you will be unemployed. I also promise all the career politicians here that I may become known in the history books as the VETO President because I will veto every bill that crosses my desk that does not look after the majority of American Taxpayers. I will veto every bill that is merely another form of welfare without accountability of the recipients. I will veto every bill that spends government's tax dollars on pet projects and on projects that benefit the minority of taxpayer vs. the majority. I will veto every bill that crosses my desk that has earmarks included. If you pass a crime bill that is what should be in that bill when it crosses my desk not earmarks to pay for airports and bridges in your home states. I demand that bills be for a specific purpose and only that purpose. If you put forth an education bill that yet again forces an unfunded mandate on the individual states, I will veto it. If the United States Congress wants the individual states to make changes to the education system then you must find a way to fund those changes. Unfunded mandates do not work. At the end of the day, the Democrats and the Republicans may override my vetoes one after the next during the next four years but I will not compromise on my promise to look after the majority of taxpayers and only the majority of taxpayers.

I know that as I stand here today there are a multitude of concerns about my foreign policies and that the world is going to spin out of control because of my lack of ability to deal internationally because of my lack of experience. However, I disagree. International relations boils down to one thing and one thing only RESPECT! I will respect all nations. I will respect established international laws and the sovereignty of all nations. However, all the nations of the world need to keep this in mind that if I am respecting your nation and its rights, all foreign nations must respect America and our rights. For to many years, America has been looked to for protection and for monetary assistance but then America is blamed for all the world's problems. We are not an evil nation and we are not responsible for all the problems of this world. Can we strive to be better world citizens – Yes but every nation can strive to be a better world citizen. I will not accept and I will not turn the other cheek when American citizens and American interests are attacked by terrorists. I will not hesitate to use military force if we are attacked. I stand here today with an olive branch and a dove – the symbols of peace. The United States of America wishes to usher in a new era of world peace but be warned if provoked and if backed into a corner I will come out swinging and I will bring down the full force and effect of the greatest military in the world on any would be terrorists.

To the Average Americans who elected me, I say thank you for the opportunity to serve you. To the Republicans and the Democrats who wish to put partisan ideals over the best interest of the American people, I am here to challenge win, lose or draw! To the political insiders here in the capital and across this great nation of ours who desire to have politics as usual, not on my watch. To the world, we are all citizens of planet earth and it is time to work together for peace but don't take that as weakness.

Thank you for your time today and now it is time for me to get to work.

The Next Four Years

The first year of my Presidency was a whirlwind. At times it was amazing, fun, and exciting. At other times it was frustrating, infuriating and more stressful than war. Luckily, I survived the first four years and I actually kind of got used to living in the fishbowl of the White House.

Over the course of my four years, I think that I was successful because I did an excellent job of selecting my advisors and I did a good job of listening to them. I am also proud to say that I can stand behind every speech that I delivered, every decision that I made and every action that I took during the four years in office.

During my first four years in office, I vetoed over 10,000 bills that landed on my desk. It was a record number of vetoes and I am proud to say that I vetoed every one of those 10,000. A lot were overridden by the two houses but I stood by my principles and vetoed those that didn't benefit the majority of taxpayers and those that included all sorts of earmarks that weren't related to the actual purpose of the bill. Plus as a result of my vetoes several career politicians were ousted from office because my vetoes put a spotlight on those politicians who were more concerned with earmarks than actual legislation that could have benefited the American taxpayer.

The issues that I decided to tackle during my years in the Oval office varied in that some were mundane, some were silly, and some were serious. The mundane and silly issues I handled with Executive Orders. The serious issues were presented as proposals to Congress. Some were actually able to get through the legislature and some were not.

Saving and Making Money

One of the first things that I changed was something that I thought was pretty silly. I shut down the Oval Office Gift Shop. I was shocked that in any given year, the Oval Office would purchase over a million dollars of souvenir type items to hand out to VIP visitors that were invited to meet with the President. The items included golf balls, golf umbrellas, picture frames, mouse pads, polo shirts, glassware, pens, key chains and etc. I ordered the entire inventory to be sold online at an auction site and I ordered no additional items to be purchased. I for one didn't see a need to hand out little mementos to visitors. After all, they weren't visiting an Amusement Park, if they were coming to the Oval Office they were coming for business purposes and they didn't need a souvenir of that visit. There were some who said I was out of touch on this issue because "it was only a million dollars". However, my argument was if one hundred lawmakers caused the government to spend "only a million dollars" and justify it by saying "its only a million dollars" then suddenly we have spent ONE HUNDRED MILLION DOLLARS and if they do that ten times a year, it suddenly becomes ONE BILLION DOLLARS. So, in my mind, each and every million dollar expenditure that I could prove wasn't absolutely necessary was one that needed to be eliminated so that I could make a difference.

The second silly thing that I changed after the souvenir business was related to the private quarters of the White House. Since I was a bachelor and didn't have children, I decided that I would open up the White House as a sort of Bed & Breakfast. Yes, I know your mouth just dropped open but it was a waste to have all those bedrooms and let them go to waste. So, for the price of one million dollars, I allowed people to book a room for a weekend for two guests. Now common sense tells you that I didn't open it up to every Tom, Dick & Harry and that every guest had to undergo a very strict background check and they were assigned a secret service agent to baby-sit them for the weekend.

Amazingly, in the first year 112 American citizens opted to pony up the one million dollars. Therefore, instead of the White House costing the American Taxpayers $ 12,814,000 (per GAO reports), the White House turned a $ 99,186,000 profit which went towards operating Air Force One which at the time was costing the United States Taxpayers approximately two hundred million dollars per year to operate. Just for the record, those people who stayed at the

White House and paid the million dollars only had access to me for one dinner and therefore, there was never the opportunity for them to seek the favor of my office.

I also thought that it was horrible that Air Force one was costing so much to run but I was thrilled that by allowing guests at the White House, we managed in turn to cut in half the cost of Air Force One. The next thing that I did was to charge reporters air fares to fly on Air Force One. Plus we at times sold individual Americans the right to fly on Air Force One. After selling seats we were able to get the total annual cost of Air Force One down to twenty five million per year. It wasn't perfect but it was definitely better.

The next proposal that I attempted to make to save the taxpayers of the United States of America millions of dollars was to propose changes to NASA. First of all, I didn't understand the billions of dollars we as a country were spending to fund space exploration. I know there are those that will say that space exploration was the hope to save the world and that a lot of technological advancements came out of NASA research. However, to me it was one giant black hole of a money pit. In addition, I couldn't wrap my head around the problems in the education system and the fact that children in the United States were going to bed hungry while we sent satellites to orbit other planets. I asked NASA to show me and the American public black and white evidence of the return on our money invested and I got a report with a whole lot of data but very little relevance. However, I was willing to let the leaders of NASA prove me wrong in what I perceived as a lack of value. So, I proposed that NASA be spun off from the United States Government and offered up in an initial public offering on the New York Stock Exchange. That is right; I wanted NASA to become a publicly traded company on the New York Stock Exchange. My thought was if they are generating all of this amazing technology that benefited mankind, why not sell all of those amazing finds and turn a profit. The caveat to my proposal was that Uncle Sam would retain 51% of NASA, Inc. and the United States always got first choice on what technology could be offered up for sale and what would remain Top Secret technology for the United States Military. NASA was spun off during my Presidency and became a successful publicly traded company.

Another idea concerned Area 51 that supposedly housed all sorts of aliens and alien technology. My first trip out of Washington DC was to go to Area 51 and have its secrets unlocked to me. My plan was that unless I really thought national security was at risk by exposing the truths about Area 51, I would recommend that the government turn the Area into an amusement park. I figured people from all over the United States and the world would be more than willing to open their wallets to visit the site and get the opportunity to see the aliens. Plus, I figured that some of the supposed Alien technology might make some really cool rides. Unfortunately, after a complete tour of the facility, I came to realize it was merely a testing ground for military technology. There wasn't anything exciting and nothing all that sexy that could be pandered to the masses as entertainment.

I also fought for the right to drill for oil and gas in some of the national parks. This of course angered the tree huggers and the liberals. What always amazed me about the liberals who seemed to yell the loudest was the fact they were the super rich and had no problem flying all over the world in their private jets and being driven around in their limos but they wanted the average American to drive around in nothing more than a glorified golf cart in order to cut our dependency on foreign oil and to save the environment. It was all nonsense. So, I made it my mission to allow for oil to be drilled for in the National Parks. However, what I fought for was extremely strict drilling regulations, that the US government would receive 80% of the profits and price controls were put in place on what the companies could sell gasoline for in the United States.

This meant that it would become illegal in the US for gas prices to increase dramatically overnight and that there would be a ceiling in place as to how high they could go. At first the oil companies balked at what I had suggested. In the end they took the deal because of greed. They knew what 20% of that oil and gas was worth and that it would more than cover their costs and produce a huge profit even if gasoline prices at the pump were strictly controlled.

Those were some of the better money saving ideas that I had and the best (with the exception of Area 51) that were able to be implemented. There were many more and I won't bore you with all of those. Let's just say I made a lot of people think I was crazy and I made a lot of people laugh with my ideas. I also made a lot of people angry and drove a couple insane with my cuts. However, at the end of the day I saved the taxpayers billions of tax dollars and I am proud of that.

Improving Government

When it came time to begin improving government, I knew the greatest improvement could come simply by solving the problems of the IRS and the United States tax system. For too many years, too many cheats had not been paying their fair share and at the same time, the IRS had become a system that was far more complex than it really needed to be. Many prior administrations had attempted to overhaul the tax code and the tax system and they had failed. However, I had some inside knowledge that helped me plan my assault on the system.

To help solve the disaster and madness of the Internal Revenue Code of the United States of America (and yes after being a CPA for so many years before becoming president – I had a ring side seat for the madness), I think I came up with a great idea on how to fix the Code and the organization that was the IRS. I turned to those on the front lines – my fellow CPAs.

What I did was I sought out volunteers from within the CPA industry. I asked for 4 from each of the 50 states. Now, the CPAs that I wanted were those who worked in the tax side of the business and I wanted those who were actually in the trenches dealing with the Average Taxpayer and the average issues.

I wasn't looking for CPAs from the TOP in terms of compensation and supposedly prestigious firms. I wasn't looking for CPAs who viewed themselves as EXPERTS or who were one of the geniuses that believed that they had the right to patent tax strategies (I won't digress to discuss such a stupid concept of being allowed to get a patent on an interpretation of a tax law but lets just say I didn't agree with it and I fully believed that the concept was not right). I wanted those CPAs who were doing the right thing and who were helping their clients within the letter of the Code.

So, after I found my volunteers, I asked them to donate one month of their time to come to Washington DC to put forth suggestions for fixing an out of control system. I didn't tell them how to do it but they did it. They divided themselves into two groups. The first week Group A worked on tax laws and Group B worked on IRS organizational changes.

The second week they flipped. The third week they presented their ideas to each other. The fourth week they voted and consolidated the reports of the two groups into one and finally they published and voted on their report.

What this group did was take existing laws that had been written in the typical government mumbo jumbo and clarified and simplified the laws. They also made a multitude of suggestions that benefited

the entire country by fixing the beast that was the IRS
organization.

The report and suggestions that came out of this conference
became the Tax Reform Act of 2017 and was welcomed by all
(with the exception of the die hard bureaucrats at the IRS). The
reforms that these individuals suggested also cut the average
taxpayers tax bill by about four thousand dollars per year and
increased tax collections by several billion dollars. How could
they decrease tax bills but increase tax collections? They were
able to close loopholes, they were able to simplify the rules so that
those taxpayers who didn't file because of the complexity of the
rules began to file once again, and they made it simpler to catch the
cheaters. Plus, they were able to make it so that those taxpayers
who had erred on the side of caution actually had black and white
rules so that they could and would take full advantage of the tax
breaks that existed which resulted in the savings.

Some of the things that came out of that conference were:

1. Definition of Reasonable Compensation – prior to this the IRS
had repeatedly refused to define what reasonable compensation
was and wasn't. Yet in every audit they were always questioning
Reasonable Compensation. It was impossible to win as a taxpayer
because there was no single definition of reasonable compensation.
It was time to define it.

2. For too many years, millions of Americans had underreported
their taxable income simply because they didn't report the income
from the sale of items on the internet. Millions of Americans were
supplementing their income that way but the companies that
owned the internet sites weren't required to issue 1099s to the
sellers. The new laws required that all sellers were to be issued
1099s regardless of the amount of sales. However, to be fair to the

American taxpayers, the conference suggested that an individual was not required to pay taxes on the first $ 2,500 in sales per year.

3. Allowed American taxpayers to contribute any amount that they desired to retirement accounts and allowed the amounts to be 100% deductible unless the individual opted to contribute to a Roth account where the contributions were not deducted but the withdrawals after retirement were not taxable. However, in order to allow the increased contributions, penalties were increased for early withdrawals.

4. In order to encourage new and future tax laws to be written in a clear and concise manner, the conference suggested that all Elected Officials be forced to undergo an IRS audit to determine that they were in compliance with all tax regulations. Amazingly, when this went to affect 55% of the federal elected officials were found to be in violation of at least one of the IRS laws. Most of the errors that were found were the result of misinterpretations of laws & regulations. Two years after this law and the new laws were written in clear and concise language when the audits of Federal Elected officials occurred only 10% were found to be in violation.

5. All members of the IRS were audited to determine and assure the American taxpayers that the enforcers were also in compliance. Again it was amazing to find out the number of IRS agents that also were not 100% in compliance.

6. Certain dreaded aspects of the Internal Revenue Code were also permanently fixed. Alternative Minimum Tax, Estate Tax and Capital Gains tax.

7. The basic overall theme of the report was simplification of rules and procedures. Once it became easier to comply with the rules, more taxpayers complied and tax collections increased.

I reconvened a similar panel each of the years that I was in the White House and each year they produced positive results. I think this was one of my best accomplishments.

The next area of government that I attempted to improve was Social Security.

One of the problems that I had always believed existed with Social Security had been the fact that instead of paying reasonable benefits based on collections, over the years that the system had existed, different groups and various politicians had added benefits that were never funded.

The following example that I am going to give is a perfect example of the math that was being used that didn't work. If it worked then the two taxpayers that I talk about would each get the same benefits but they didn't because the system was paying out benefits that they shouldn't.

Mr. X and Mr. Y have lived next door to each other and they have both worked for 35 years at the same company and both made exactly the same amount of money and paid the same amount of taxes over the years. Mr. X remained single his entire life and Mr. Y was married and he and his wife decided when they got married that she would remain at home and not work. After working and paying into the system the same amount of money, Mr. X received two thousand dollars a month in benefits at retirement time while Mr. Y received three thousand dollars a month because his wife also received a check that was one half of Mr. Y's amount. Then Mr. X & Mr. Y die on the same day but Mr. Y's wife continues to receive two thousand dollars a month until she dies. Let's say Mr. X is retired for 20 years, he collects four hundred and eighty thousand dollars while Mr. Y collects seven hundred and twenty thousand dollars. Not to mention the benefits that Mrs. Y continues to collect after Mr. Y's death. Yet Social Security collected the same amount from both taxpayers when they were paying into the system. If Social Security could afford to pay out the higher benefits to Mr. Y and his wife, why didn't Mr. X get the higher amount? The system didn't pay the higher amounts to Mr. X because the system couldn't afford to pay them. In addition, Mr. & Mrs. Y made a CHOICE for her to not work so why were they rewarded and Mr. X punished?

The excess benefits were NEVER funded and should not have been paid. It was a simple fact however; they were paid because it was a form of welfare. What should have happened was that if a couple chose for the wife not to work then the husband should have paid a surcharge during his working career in order to provide benefits to his wife upon his retirement. In addition, in order to provide benefits to his widow following his death, Mr. Y should have had a deduction from his monthly benefit to purchase a life insurance policy to pay benefits following his death. I know what I am saying is a radical idea – if you choose for a spouse not to work then guess what it isn't every other American's responsibility to provide for your spouse's retirement instead it is your responsibility.

Another prime example of an idea that never made sense about Social Security was when it was decided to pay disability benefits to the minor children of recipients who are on SS Disability. Now I know you are thinking that that sounds pretty damn harsh but hear me out. The following example illustrates my frustration with the system.

Mr. & Mrs. A have two children under the age of 18 when Mrs. A suffers a stroke and becomes disabled. Mrs. A had paid into Social Security for over 20 years. She deserves her disability. However, the Social Security Administration takes 18 months to approve it. The entire 18 months that they are waiting on disability, Mr. A continues working as an attorney making over $ 200,000 per year. Prior to her stroke, Mrs. A had only earned $15,000 per year. The family never goes without food, never loses their home etc during the 18 months. However, when she finally receives her back disability payments, Social Security pays her two children several thousand dollars in back disability payments as well. WHY?? First of all those children have a father who can and does support them and they were not ill affected by the lack of money during the 18 months. Once again benefits were being paid to people who didn't need it and the benefits had never been paid for by the parent when she had paid into the system.

I fought long and hard for these changes because I knew that these were crucial to the survival of Social Security.

Now I will say that a lot of people were angered by these suggestions but once they really looked at what I was saying and that the ideas would shore up Social Security the majority of taxpayers agreed with my plans. The ones that never did agree were the ones who no longer got to take advantage of Social Security.

The final program that I fought long and hard to improve was the welfare system. As I had said during my inauguration speech, it was time for compassion with accountability. It was time that those on welfare learned a different life. This ended up being a harder fight then tax reform and Social Security reform. In the end I failed every attempt that I made during my first term. The career politicians just wanted it to be left as is. I couldn't get the votes. However, I truly believed that there were lots of opportunities to improve the system. I brought up numerous changes each and every year for 8 years and I failed the first four years. During my second 4 years I was able to get some changes in place thanks to more independent candidates reaching congress.

Terrorists

During my terms in office, the United States of America was lucky in so much as there were no terrorist attacks against America or American interests. I credit this first and foremost to the brave men and women that serve out country in the military and the intelligence services.

The intelligence services were able to stop several attempts because they were doing their jobs and I didn't get in their way. They didn't have a blank check to do just anything and they were accountable but the systems in place worked.

I would also like to think that because my Presidency truly concentrated on a lot of domestic problems that also made a difference. I didn't spend my years in office trying to be the answer to all of the world's problems. I was careful in what I said and how I said it when I was on the world stage. In the years prior to my Presidency, most if not all of the Presidents worked extremely hard to bring peace to the Middle East. Specifically they tried to broker peace deals for Israel. Yet, it never truly worked. I just decided that because the fighting had been going on over there for centuries just what made me think that I was going to change it in 2016. How was I supposed to come up with some great idea that had never been thought of before my time in the Oval Office? I publicly stated when asked that I believed that peace should be found at all possible costs but I certainly couldn't effect change just because I was the President of the United States of America. Maybe I was being too simplistic and maybe I was being too realistic but that was who I was.

On a few times world tensions were elevated and I did my best to offer my version of diplomacy when and where I could. When and where American interests were threatened I warned that if we were brought into the problem then we would solve it by military force if required. On more than one occasion, I did deploy the Special Forces to solve problems.

In closing, after eight long years in office I thanked God that America was not attacked and I never had to experience leadership under such trying times.

My Second Term

At about the end of the second year of any Presidential term, the sitting President typically begins the process of actively seeking their second term in office. In reality from day one they are campaigning for their second term. However, me being me, I never once made a decision that was based on whether or not it would effect a second term because I never figured I would serve a second term.

However, somehow, I managed to strike a nerve and a group of very wealthy Americans who agreed with my ideals and the changes that I was able to effect and tried to make happen during my first three years in office decided that I should seek a second term and they managed to get me on the ballot.

Once again, I went about the campaign completely different than anyone else. In fact, I never campaigned. Instead I just kept working the entire time that the D & the R candidates slugged it out. They drug my name and reputation down into the mud but I didn't allow myself to be drug down into the mud. They tried to goad me into participating in their debates. Yet I never went there. Then at some point, the strategists for the D candidate and the strategists for the R candidate realized that their candidates were agreeing on too many points about me and they began to worry that nobody was going to be able to tell them apart. So, they decided to turn on each other and they pulled out all of the stops.

The R candidate tried to compare the D candidate to me and the D candidate tried to compare the R candidate to me. Eventually, they realized that once again they weren't getting anywhere with that strategy and as a result they switched to their usual tactics and began to dig up the dirt and search the closets for skeletons. Luckily, for me I had no skeletons in my closet but the two other candidates had more than enough.

As a result, I beat out the D & R who ran. I was shocked, thrilled and proud of myself. My second term pretty much was a repeat of my first. I fought the fight that I thought was mine to fight on behalf of the average American taxpayer. I continued to veto what I thought was government waste. However, during my second term the two houses of the legislature had many more independents like me as opposed to the Democrats & Republicans. I found myself with much more support and I was able to further many of my new agendas.

MY BIGGEST CONTROVERSIES
HOOKERS AND DRUGS!

Early, in my second term, I did an interview that when it was published the next morning, caused so much controversy that I thought for a brief moment the villagers were going to gather at the gates of the White House with pitchforks and torches to tar and feather the monster (meaning me) and impeach me by impaling me on their pitchforks. While I was accurately quoted in the headline that I wanted to legalize and tax both prostitution and drugs, nobody bothered to actually read my plans for legalization and as a result everyone of the Moral Majority went ballistic. Not surprisingly, even those that claimed to have read my proposal either read what they wanted to read into it or just were so angry with me that they didn't give a damn to tell the truth about my plan.

Anyway my plans were actually to legalize both just to make it go away. I know you are thinking. What? How do you make something go away by legalizing it right? Well, here was my plan. The federal government would legalize both hookers and drugs. However, the conditions of legal use of drugs and the legal brothels would be both highly regulated and highly taxed and illegal use of either would become even more criminal with substantially higher penalties to the point where nobody in their right mind would do them regardless of whether they were legal or illegal.

The regulations that I wanted were as follows:

Each entity had to be operated as a corporation and needed a minimum of ten million dollars in capitalization per each location where the corporation did business.

Each entity had to carry a one billion dollar liability insurance policy per location where the corporation did business.

Each owner of the entity had to have no previous felony convictions and had to be current on all tax liabilities. Each owner would be subject to annual IRS audits.

Each employee of the entities had to be provided a health insurance policy and a 401K plan and the entity was required to match all 401K contributions.

No entity could operate in any community or state without the consent of 90% of the registered voters in the community.

Anyone selling drugs and/or prostituting outside of the guidelines as established and found guilty in a court of law would be executed.

To be a customer of the establishments, a person must be 21 years of age and of sound mind. Plus, nobody that has been convicted of a felony could be a customer of the establishments. Finally, no customer could be on public assistance. Customers in violation of the rules would also face a death penalty. Also, customers would be required to pay a fee of a thousand dollars to the US government for the issuance of a license to participate in the activities.

In the event that a user of drugs is convicted of committing a crime while under the influence (including driving under the influence) the customer will also face the death penalty. Plus the entity would be liable for all damages caused by the customer who was under the influence at the time of the customer's actions.

Finally, the tax rate for the entities in question would be an automatic 50% of the net profits and all entities would be audited on an annual basis by the IRS. The entities would be required to pay an annual audit fee to the IRS of twenty-five thousand dollars for the privilege of being audited.

Now obviously some of the regulations that I proposed were outrageous and there were more than a few raised eyebrows by what I suggested. However, nobody ever made headway in solving the two issues so I thought what the heck why not make a suggestion that was out there. Something needed done. Personally, I have no problem allowing communities to set their own moral standards i.e. allow prostitution or allow drug sales/use. However, just because some people wanted to allow it; it didn't mean everyone should have to tolerate it or be around it. Also, the penalties that had been law certainly weren't regulating the activities out of existence so if it wasn't wanted by 90% of the population (see community vote regulation) then why not invoke the ultimate penalty (death) to discourage it.

It never happened but I certainly stirred up debate and tougher laws were enacted that did help ebb the trades. Specifically, those buying drugs and the johns soliciting the hookers had to face penalties and punishments that were on par with the drug dealers and the hookers.

SCANDAL

I am proud to say that I made it through my first four years without any scandals personally or for any of members of my administration. Unfortunately, I cannot say that for my second term. During my second term, the gentleman that I appointed as my Secretary of Defense became a huge embarrassment. Drugs, alcohol, women and bribery were involved. It was splashed all over the tabloids before I even knew what was going on. People within my administration had decided to hide the matter from me because at the time I was busy trying to fight a battle with the two houses over the budget for 2021. When the matter did become public I acted swiftly and with purpose. I immediately fired all that were involved in the scandal and ordered the Attorney General to prosecute to the full extent of the law. I have always been harsh on myself on this matter because I have always thought that I should have known what was going on in my administration. Even though I honestly didn't know what was going on, I knew that as a prior President said "the bucks stops here!" so no excuses.

The second scandal to this day baffles me to no end. A very good friend of mine from high school who had become a great actress was involved in the scandal. My friend had graduated and left our small town headed for the bright lights of Broadway and had never looked back. She had won Tony awards, Emmy Awards and even an Oscar by the time that I had entered the White House. After I had been elected, she had once again gotten in contact with me and we picked up our friendship like we had never been apart. She would often times join me at the White House as the Hostess for diplomatic parties. We weren't really dating because it just wouldn't be possible for the President of the United States of America to date – at least not in the traditional sense. However, I enjoyed her company and she enjoyed mine (or so I thought). After my 5th year in office, she suddenly broke off all contact with me and disappeared. Several months later she showed up in Hollywood at a press conference stating that she was pregnant with my child and that I was denying that the child was mine and that I had even told her to have an abortion. I was shocked because she and I had never had any such conversation and prior to the news conference I had no idea that she was pregnant. The entire world looked at me as though I was a liar and scumbag. It was truly the worst moment of my life. I denied that I had ever had the conversation and stated that child could be mine but that she had never told me about the pregnancy before the press conference. A month later she showed up very much NOT pregnant and at another press conference she stated that I had sent the Secret Service after her and that they had snatched her baby from her and had threatened her life. This was bizarre and beyond comprehension to me as to why she was doing this to me. Finally, after three months, the FBI was able to prove that she had never been pregnant and that everything had occurred because of her drug use that was fueled by her latest boyfriend some thirty years younger than her. I knew that I was vindicated but to this day there are those conspiracy people (the ones that don't believe that the United States ever landed on the moon and the ones that think the United States government staged the attacks on 9-11-01) that believe that I had the Secret Service snatch my child from the actress. Some even believe that I did it to send my child to be raised by aliens.

MISC.

My entire Presidency (both the first term and the second term) wasn't entirely a fight with Congress. There were also some highlights that I am proud of that didn't exactly change the world but I was proud that I did them.

As a veteran of the United States Armed Forces, I was always very proud of our military. I also knew how nice it was to know that those in charge were proud and totally committed to support the troops at the bottom of the food chain. So, during my years in the Oval Office, I attended every graduation ceremony of each of the US Military Academies and I was there to be one of the first people to salute our newest officers. I wanted them to know that the Commander in Chief recognized the huge achievement of their graduation and to wish them well. I also made sure that I visited military installations all over the world and actually took time to speak with members of our military at every level of the ranks. I didn't just want to hear from those at the top, I wanted to know what everyone thought and what they needed help with and I always went to bat to fix their problems when and where I could.

My hometown annually celebrates the US Constitution in September. Every year, I would go home during that week and participate in the celebration and help in every way that I could. It was great that as President I could point the spotlight on the Constitution and remind everyone just how important it will always be to our country.

I also had the honor of nominating two individuals to the United States Supreme Court. As usual when it comes time for a President to nominate to the Supreme Court, it instantly became a debate on Abortion. The thing about that issue being so important in the nominee debate always amazed me because it had become THE deciding factor in the selection process. Presidents had to choose the candidate that was right for their view on abortion and then the review committee spent hours and hours grilling the candidate on that one issue.

Supreme Court justices hear so many more cases that have nothing to do with abortion yet every nominee is dissected over abortion – an issue that I believe will never be settled in this country. What we as Americans should be focused on when it comes to Supreme Court nominees is what is the person's knowledge of Constitutional Law and whether or not the person exhibits sound and fair judgment.

I never asked either person that I nominated what they thought of abortion but rather I asked if they could make their decisions solely on the rule of law established by the Constitution. I also wanted to know what they thought of judges who legislate from the bench. Both of the candidates refused to answer the abortion question personally but spoke about the Constitution and that Supreme Court Justices existed to interpret the laws not create laws. Both passed the review process and both became Justices. I am proud now after all these years to say that they both had stellar careers. I am especially proud of the fact that one of my best friends and my own personal attorney who I nominated (in spite of the fact that she had never served as a Judge (Federal, State or Local)) managed to impress the review committee and get their approval to become a Justice and that she eventually became the first female Chief Justice.

I am also happy to say that over my eight years, I met a lot of wonderful people of all ages and types all over this country who inspired me and who challenged me. I was proud to serve them but even more proud to meet them and hear their stories. America is a great country with great people and I got to experience it all thanks to the fact that I became President of the United States of America.

Finally as I left office, I was content with what I had accomplished. I had become President without having to spend hundreds of millions of dollars. I didn't have to become a robot that could only speak the party line of partisan politics. I could actually think for myself and do what I believed was right for the majority of taxpaying citizens. I was an Average American President and damn proud of it.

Chapter Ten – Post Presidency

After eight years in Washington DC, I anxiously awaited my return to Louisville, Ohio and retirement. While I had only been gone eight years, I felt as though I had been gone for over eighty years. In fact when I went into the Oval Office, I only had a few grey hairs but when I left I don't think there was a single brown hair left – my entire head of hair was grey. The weight and pressure of that job was beyond belief but I had no regrets.

When I first left office every publishing house constantly contacted me wanting me to publish my memoirs. I just never did it because as I stated earlier I just never thought that I had anything all that important to say. More than one publisher and several literary agents went crazy trying to contact me and woo me into writing the memoirs. They would come and visit and take me to lunch or dinner only to leave my small hometown with a NO from me. One guy in particular came every week for the first three years because he told me that he was going to wear me down until he got a yes out of me. At the first dinner that we had, he told me he didn't drink alcohol and he didn't smoke because he was into running marathons and he loved to live healthy. At the end of the three years he was smoking two packs a day and drank several

Vodka tonics every meeting. No matter what he proposed my answer was always no. If he is still alive – I would say sorry that I didn't do this sooner and that I couldn't have helped you out.

When I left office, I received my Presidential Pension plus an allowance for office staff. I accepted the pension and turned down the office allowance. Once again, my goal was to save the United States taxpayers some money. However, this did mean that I was somewhat slow in answering the thousands of letters and emails that I received but I did work on them on a regular basis and did my best to answer them. My sisters who were retired by that time also did a lot of volunteering to help me. I also was able to get some high school students who were required to do volunteer work to come in and help as well. They loved being able to pad their resumes with "aide to ex-President of the United States of America."

I also received lots of offers to speak all over the country in my retirement. I know that a lot of previous Presidents had charged some really big speaking fees in the past and really supplemented their income (in fact they became stinking rich) with their speaking fees. However, since I was receiving a paycheck courtesy of the American taxpayer, I didn't feel right taking a fee to speak to them. After all, I figured if an American Taxpayer wanted to hear what I had to say bad enough, I would say it for free (with the exception of my travel fees). I even went so far as to once speak at a cookout for 25 people. The only thing was sometimes, when I would speak, I would speak my mind and at times, I ended up making my hosts angry, but that was just me being me. I didn't and wouldn't draft my speeches to suit anyone but myself.

The thing that I am most proud of during my retirement years was the fact that I went back to my days of being a volunteer in my community. I was able to work with a variety of some of the old charities that I worked with prior to becoming President and some new charities. It was also nice that as a former President of the United States, I was able to use that to get some great donations for the charities. I would never have wanted to use my status for my personal benefit but I wasn't ashamed of milking it for everything that it was worth on behalf of my charities.

I was also proud to say that on numerous occasions I was called upon by the sitting Presidents to assist the US on diplomatic missions when the President just couldn't go himself. However, I was never asked to do this by any of the Presidents that came after me that identified himself or herself as a Republican or a Democrat because they knew I wouldn't toe a party line.

When I first left office I tried my best not to speak out about the subsequent President's policies or actions. However, on a few occasions, I found I just couldn't help myself. I had fought so hard to do what was best for the Average Taxpayer and the majority of taxpayers as opposed to special interests and I had tried my very best to balance the budget and cut waste and when I saw partisan politics kissing the butts of the special interests or wasting taxpayer dollars, I just had to speak out. I will say I pride myself on sticking to the issues without personally attacking the person on the occasions when I spoke out.

The greatest part about retirement was going home and enjoying my life. I reconnected with family and friends and caught up on my reading. Life was good and I was truly content with what I had done and where I was.

And then the years went by . . . and here I am tonight December 9th, 2065. . and all that I have to say is that as I have sat here on my 100th birthday writing this book, I have had the chance to remember my ancestors who gave me so much to help shape me into the man that I became and the man that I still am. I have also had the opportunity to remember so many events which also shaped me and left scars and left happy memories.

I have also been able to reconcile the good things and the bad things that I have done and lived through. I now know that my parents were my parents. They had their good points and their bad points but in the end they were my parents and they loved me and I loved them.

I also think back to when I was a child and I learned the following prayer to say before bed each night:

> Now I lay myself down to sleep
> I pray to the Lord my soul to keep
> If I die before I wake
> I pray the Lord my soul to take.

POST SCRIPT

December 10th, 2065 – Shady Oaks Nursing Home – Morning Report – 5th Floor Nursing Station – Canton, Ohio.

Just like every other shift change at every nursing facility in the world, the outgoing head nurse exchanged details of the prior shift with the head nurse of the incoming shift. The census of patients and all important patient information is passed in order to facilitate the treatment and care of the patients.

On this day, Nurse Jackie Smith began her briefing of the previous night for Nurse Regina Johnson, head nurse of the day shift for Shady Oaks Nursing Home.

Jackie: "We had a death last night"

Regina: "Really – who?"

Jackie: "Jay B. Barton – Room # 585"

Regina: "Oh that's a shame – hasn't he been here forever?"

Jackie: "Yes, he has been here since 1991 when he returned from Operation Desert Storm at the age of 25. Poor man was the victim of some weird Iraqi chemical in Saudi Arabia. He was the only member of his Army unit to be seriously affected by the chemical. All the other members suffered just flu like symptoms. However, for some reason the chemical only affected Mr. Barton and only affected his mind – never his body. For the last seventy five years he just lay in that bed mumbling all sorts of stories over and over. Talked a lot about the President of the United States"

Regina: "Yes it was all very sad!"

Jackie: "At least he is finally at peace after 75 years."

THE END